W9-BVG-654

Dear A.J, May these stories feed your imagination, and set your mind on believing that you can be and/or do anything that is possible.

May you enjoy them while you embark on wonderful, fantastic, imaginative, and creative adventures every time that they are read to you, or when you are able to read them yourself.

I wish you + your family long + happy years. Love, Chencha.

08/07/04

This book belongs to

Abraham Alvarez, Jr.
A/K/A A.J.
08/07/04

Contributors

Illustrated by
Alison Atkins, Andrew Geeson, Andy Everitt Stewart,
Anglea Kincaid, Anna Cynthia Leplar, Caroline Davis,
Claire Henley, Claire Mumford, Daniel Howarth,
Dorothy Clark, Elaine Keary, Frank Endersby,
Georgia Birkett, Gillian Roberts, Jacqueline East,
Jacqueline Mair, Jan Lewis, Jane Molineaux,
Jane Swift, Jane Tattersfield, Jessica Stockham,
Jo Brown, Julie Nicholson, Karen Perrins, Kate Aldous,
Kate Davies, Linda Worrell, Liz Pichon, Louise Gardner,
Maggie Downer, Mario Capaldi, Martin Grant, Nicola Evans,
Paula Martyr, Peter Rutherford, Piers Harper, Rebecca Elgar,
Rikki O'Neill, Rory Tyger, Sara Walker, Scott Rhodes,
Serena Feneziani, Sheila Moxley, Stephanie Boey, Sue Clarke,
Terry Burton, Pauline Siewart, Lorna Bannister

Written by
Nicola Baxter, Janet Allison Brown, Andrew Charman, Jillian
Harker, Heather Henning, Alistair Hedley, Claire Keen,
Ronne Randall, Lesley Rees, Caroline Repchuk, Kay Barnes,
Gaby Goldsack, Aneurin Rhys, Louisa Somerville, Derek Hall,
Marilyn Tolhurst, Alison Morris, Nicola Edwards,
Jackie Andrews

BEDTIME TALES

A Keepsake Treasury

Every effort has been made to acknowledge the contributors to this book. If we have made any errors, we will be pleased to rectify them in future editions.

This is a Parragon Publishing Book
This edition published in 2003

Parragon Publishing
Queen Street House
4 Queen Street
Bath BA1 1HE, UK

Design and project management by Aztec Design

Page make-up by Mik Martin and Caroline Reeves

ISBN 1-40542-397-8
Printed in China

BEDTIME
TALES

A Keepsake Treasury
p

Contents

One Stormy Night

It was Patch's first night outside in his smart new kennel. He snuggled down on his warm blanket and watched as the skies grew dark. Before long he fell fast asleep. As he slept, big spots of rain began to fall. A splash of water dripped from the kennel roof on to his nose.

Just then, there was a great crash and a bright flash of light lit up the sky. Patch woke with a start and was on his feet at once, growling and snarling. "It's just a silly old storm," he told himself. "Nothing to scare a fearless farm dog like me!" But as the lightning flashed again, he saw a great shadow looming against the barn. Patch gulped. Whatever could it be? Patch began to bark furiously, trying to act braver than he felt. Next time the lightning flashed, there was no sign of the shadow. "I soon scared that monster away!" he thought.

But as Patch settled back down in his cozy kennel, the sky outside lit up once more, and there, standing in the doorway, towered the monster!

"Are you alright?" asked Mommy, and licked Patch on the ear.

"A fearless farm dog like me?" said Patch. "Of course I am!" But as the storm raged on, he snuggled up close to her all the same!

Morag the Witch

Morag was just an ordinary witch—until the day she enrolled for a course of advanced spell casting at the Wizard, Witch and Warlock Institute of Magic. For that was where she met Professor Fizzlestick. Now Professor Fizzlestick was a very wise old man indeed. Morag, on the other hand, was a very vain young witch who didn't know as much as she thought she did. She could turn people into frogs if they really deserved it, and do other simple spells like that, but she still had a lot to learn. The problem was, Morag thought she was the most perfect little witch in the whole wide world.

Morag's adventure started on her very first day at school. At the beginning of the day, after all the young witches and wizards had made friends and met the teachers, they were called in one by one to talk to Professor Fizzlestick.

"Now, young Morag Bendlebaum,

I taught both your mother and your father," said the professor in a very serious voice, "and a very fine witch and wizard they turned out to be, too. So, what kind of witch do you think you are going to be?"

Without giving this any thought at all, Morag blurted out, "I'm better than my parents, and I'm probably better than you!"

This answer surprised even Morag, for although she thought this was true, she didn't actually mean to say it.

"Don't be surprised by your answers," said Professor Fizzlestick, "there is a truth spell in this room, and whatever you truly believe you must say. And I must say you appear to have a very high opinion of yourself. Why don't you tell me what makes you so very good?"

"I'm clever," said Morag, "and I'm good, and I'm always right."

"But what about your dark side?" said Professor Fizzlestick.

"I am very sorry to disappoint you," replied Morag quite seriously. "I'm afraid I simply don't have a dark side."

"Well in that case I would like you to meet someone very close to you," said Professor Fizzlestick with a smile on his lips.

Morag looked over to where Professor Fizzlestick pointed, and was startled to see on the sofa next to her... herself!

As Morag stared open-mouthed with astonishment, the professor explained that if, as she believed, she was without a dark side, then there was absolutely nothing to worry about. "If, however," he continued, "you have deceived yourself, then I'm afraid you are in for a few surprises."

With that the professor dismissed them both from the room and told them to get to know each other. As Morag and her dark side stood outside the professor's room, Morag's dark side jumped and whooped for joy.

"At last," she cried, "I'm free. I don't have to sit and listen to you telling me what's right all day; I don't have to keep persuading you to choose the biggest slice of cake before your brother—in fact, I don't, I repeat don't, have to do anything that you tell me, at all."

So saying, she broke into a run and rushed down the corridor, knocking over chairs and bumping into other little witches and wizards along the way. Morag was horrified. She would have to follow her dark side and stop her from causing trouble. Morag chased after her dark side and finally caught up with her at the chocolate machine. "Don't eat all that chocolate," cried Morag. "You know it's bad for your teeth and will ruin your appetite for lunch!"

"Tsk!" scoffed her dark side. "You might not want any chocolate but I certainly do!" And with that she ran off once more, dropping chocolate on to the freshly polished floor as well as pushing a big piece into her mouth.

Just then, the bell sounded for lunch. Although Morag felt she ought to find her dark side, she also knew that the bell was a command to go to the dining hall, and she mustn't disobey it. Morag sat down to lunch next to her friend, Topaz. She was just about to tell her what had happened, when she saw that Topaz was not eating her vegetables! Morag scolded Topaz for this, and gave her a lecture on eating healthily.

Topaz stared at Morag in amazement, then peered closely at her. "What's happened to you?" she asked, so Morag explained what had happened in Professor Fizzlestick's office.

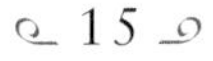

Then she declared, "It's the best thing that has ever happened to me. I thought I was good before, but now I'm even better. I never want my dark side back again, but we must lock her up so that she can do no harm."

Topaz agreed that they must find her dark side, but secretly hoped that she and Morag would be re-united. Morag wasn't Morag without her dark side. So, after lunch, Morag went for her first lesson of the afternoon. When she got to the classroom she discovered her dark side was already there, busy preparing spells! Morag's dark side had already prepared a "turning a nose into an elephant's trunk" spell and a "turning skin into dragons' scales" spell and was just finishing off a "turning your teacher into stone" spell!

Morag suddenly heard a trumpeting noise from the back of the classroom. The wizard twins, Denzil and Dorian Dillydally, had sprouted huge grey trunks down to the ground where their noses had been. As Morag rushed over to her dark side to make her change them back, she tripped over a creature crouched on the floor. It looked like a dragon and it was wearing a purple and white spotted dress last seen on Bettina Bumblebag. Morag's dark side was casting spells all over the place. "Oh, why doesn't the teacher stop her!" cried Morag to Topaz. But as I'm sure you have guessed by now—Nice Miss Chuckle was entirely turned to stone from head to foot!

Just then Professor Fizzlestick walked into the classroom. Morag pointed to her dark side, still making spells at the front of the classroom.

"Lock her up immediately," Morag begged the professor.

"I'm afraid that you are the only one who can do that," said the wise old man. "The two of you are inseparable and you need each other. Without your dark side you would be unbearable and without you she is dreadful. Have I your permission to lock her back inside you?"

Even though Morag didn't want any part of her dark side back, she agreed reluctantly. Her dark side instantly disappeared, and Morag felt... wonderful! Oh, it was so good to be back to normal, to be basically good, but occasionally mischievous.

"Thank you," said Morag to the professor. "I think I've learned something very valuable today."

"There is good and bad in everyone," replied the professor, "even the most perfect of witches."

Morag and Topaz went back to the classroom to undo all the bad things Morag's dark side had done, but on the way they both felt a huge urge for a snack, so they stopped at the chocolate machine first!

Princess Petal

Princess Petal lives in a shiny white castle surrounded by beautiful grounds, filled with pretty flowers and colorful butterflies. The Princess's best friend is Sparkle, a sweet little puppy. Every morning, he helps the princess to choose her dress.

"Which one today?" she asks.

Sparkle stands next to a pretty yellow one, wags his tail and barks.

"Perfect," says the Princess.

Then they play games in the grounds. They love to run and jump and play "catch the ball".

Today, Princess Petal is very excited. She has just received an invitation to a special party—a ball at the palace.

“The Prince is very handsome,” Petal says to her puppy. “I must look my best.”

She slips on a beautiful pink dress, trimmed with jewels and satin ribbons. On her feet are dainty gold slippers. Then Petal opens her jewelry box and takes out a pair of crystal earrings and a diamond tiara.

She places the tiara carefully on her head—now she can go off to the ball in her beautiful horse-drawn carriage.

As the Princess and Sparkle enter the crowded ballroom, everyone gasps in delight. Then the handsome Prince takes the Princess’s hand.

“You are the loveliest lady here,” he says. “May I have this dance?”

“Of course, Your Majesty!” says the Princess.

Princess Petal is the happiest girl in the whole kingdom.

Staying at Grandma's

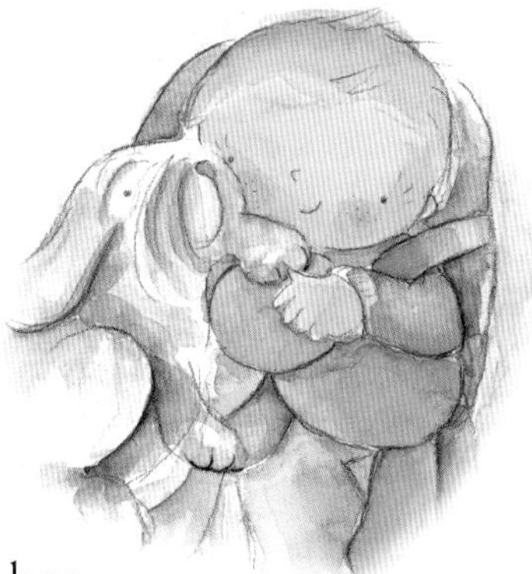

Jack hugged his teddy bear tightly, while Mom packed his slippers and pajamas into a bag.

"Why can't I come with you?" he asked.

"Dad and I have to go away for one night," said Mom. "You're going to stay with Gran and Grandad. They can't wait to see you."

"But I'll be scared without you and Dad," whispered Jack.

"Don't worry," said Mom. "You'll have such a good time, you won't want to come home!"

Later that day, when Gran and Grandad opened their front door, Holly, their little dog, peeped through Gran's legs and wagged her tail with excitement. But soon, it was time for Jack to say goodbye to his mom and dad. Jack felt really sad. He didn't want them to leave. He hugged his mom tightly. "I'll miss you," he said.

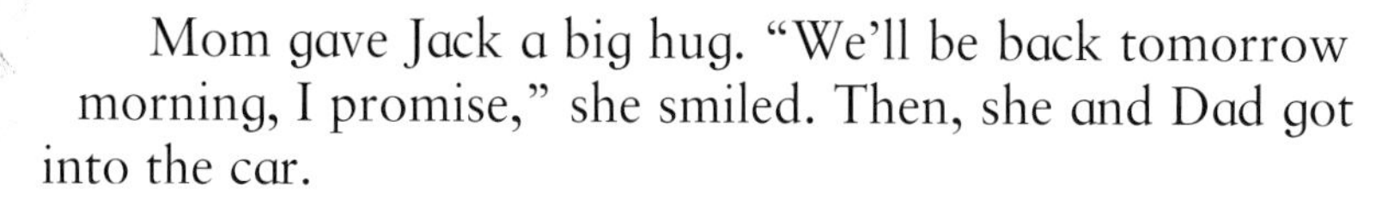

Mom gave Jack a big hug. "We'll be back tomorrow morning, I promise," she smiled. Then, she and Dad got into the car.

As they drove away, Jack waved until he couldn't see the car anymore. His eyes filled with tears. "Come on, Jack," said Gran, giving him a big cuddle. "We're going to have such a good time. Guess where Grandad's taking us this afternoon?" Grandad gave him a tissue.

"Um... I don't know," he sniffed. Just then, Holly came bounding over. "Hello, Holly," said Jack, looking more cheerful. He rubbed her big, floppy ears. Jack loved Holly and, just for tonight, he could pretend she was his dog.

"Grandad," asked Jack, "where are we going this afternoon?"

"It's a surprise," said Grandad. "But we'll need the car. Why don't we give it a good clean?" So, Grandad gave Jack a big, yellow sponge and a pail of soapy water. Soon, bubbles filled the air. They even went on Holly's nose!

Just then, Gran called to Jack from the kitchen. "I'm going to make a lovely picnic to take with us," said Gran. "Would you like to help me, Jack?"

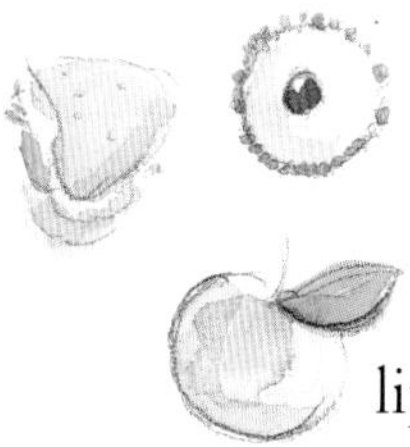

Jack nodded. At home, he liked to help his mom, too. "Grandad likes ham sandwiches, and I like cheese sandwiches," said Gran. "What's your favorite?"

"Chocolate spread sandwiches!" said Jack, licking his lips. "Can we take something for Holly, too?"

"Of course," said Gran, smiling. "She can have one of her favorite crunchy dog biscuits."

When the car was clean and the picnic was ready, Jack and Grandad carefully packed everything for their trip into the trunk.

Then, Gran strapped Jack into his car seat, Holly jumped into the back of the car and they all set off.

"Here we are," said Grandad. "The park."

"Great!" said Jack. He couldn't wait to get out and explore. They soon found the perfect place for their picnic. Jack hungrily ate his chocolate spread sandwiches.

Afterwards, Grandad took Jack and Holly for a walk in the woods, while Gran had a little nap. On the way, Jack saw a playground. "Can we go there, Grandad?" he asked.

"Of course, we can," said Grandad. First, Grandad pushed Jack on the swings and then watched him zoom down the slide.

"Wheee!" cried Jack. "This is great fun!" Soon, he was laughing and playing with all the other children, while Grandad watched, just like Jack's mom and dad would do.

When it was time to go home, Gran packed up the picnic things and Grandad put them back in the car. Jack was very tired and soon fell asleep. What a fun day they'd had!

That evening, Gran made Jack a special dinner—sausages and mash, followed by apple pie and ice cream.

Afterwards, they watched Jack's favorite television program, then it was time for bed. As Jack settled himself in bed, with his teddy bear beside him, Grandad asked him what story he would like.

"Mom usually reads me this one," said Jack, picking up a book and handing it to Grandad.

"Once upon a time… " began Grandad. Jack knew the story off by heart. It was nice to hear it again, and soon he was drifting off to sleep. It was just like being at home.

When Jack woke up, he couldn't understand why his room felt so strange. Then, he remembered. He was staying with Gran and Grandad!

"Breakfast time, Jack," said Gran, as she came to help him get dressed. "Did you sleep well?"

"Yes, thank you, Gran," he said.

For breakfast, Gran cooked Jack a boiled egg with toast, and he had milk and fresh orange juice. Delicious!

Jack helped Gran to clear away the breakfast things and do the washing up. Then he helped Gran to pack his bag, ready for when Mom and Dad came to collect him.

Holly and Jack had great fun chasing each other round the yard. Then he saw his mom and dad arrive and ran to meet them. He gave them both a giant hug.

"Jack!" cried Mom. "Have you had a really good time?"

"Yes," laughed Jack. "We went to the park and had a picnic, and I played on a slide, and had chocolate sandwiches, and we took Holly for a walk... and Grandad read me my favorite story. Please can I stay again?"

Everyone laughed and Holly barked.

"Of course, you can!" said Mom and Dad.

The Soccer Fairy

Georgina loved to play soccer, but she had one problem. "I'm fed up with these silly wings," she said to the wise fairy, Sparkle. "They just get in the way. I don't want to be a fairy!" said Georgina, and stamped off to play soccer with the elves. The soccer game was very rough. The ball bounced around the field and, quite often, off the field! Sometimes it went up into the trees. Two birds who were trying to build their nest got very fed up.

Georgina flew up to get it. "Perhaps my wings can be useful after all," she thought. She looked round quickly, hoping no one had seen her.

But Barry, the elf, had and he couldn't wait to tell the fairies. "Ah," nodded the wise fairy. "I knew she would use her wings sooner or later."

The next time Georgina played soccer, the game was rougher than ever. One elf kicked the ball so hard it flew into the tree and hit the birds' nest. This time there was an egg in it! The egg began to topple, but none of the elves noticed, they were far too busy arguing with the referee. So Georgina flew up and, just in time, caught the egg before it hit the ground.

"Thank you," said the mommy bird, as she tucked the egg back under her. "But please, be more careful when you play soccer!"

Next time she played soccer, Georgina checked the tree first. The mommy bird was away. "Good!" she thought. "She can't complain this time." But, thanks to a naughty elf, the soccer ball knocked into the birds' nest. A small bundle of feathers tumbled out. It was a baby bird!

Georgina spotted it and, quick as lightning, she flew up to catch him. Gently, she held him in her arms and flew back to the nest. When he was safely inside she sprinkled him with fairy dust to keep him from further harm. Just then the mommy bird came back.

"I shall tell everyone about your kindness," she said, as her baby snuggled under her feathers. "And, as you're such a good fairy, will you be baby Beak's godmother?"

"Oh, thank you! I'd be delighted!" said Georgina.

When they heard the news, the other fairies were very proud of her.

"Perhaps it's not so bad being a fairy after all," grinned Georgina, happily.

Missing Mouse

In some ways, Molly Mouse was just like her brother and sisters. She had soft, pink ears and a cute, little nose. But, in other ways, she was very different...

Milly, Max, and Baby Mouse were very tidy, but Molly was really, really messy! Her whiskers were never clean and her paws were always grubby. And, everywhere Molly went, she left a messy muddle behind her!

After breakfast, Milly and Max never forgot to make their beds. Each and every morning, they threw out their old bedding and made new beds with fresh, clean hay. But Molly wasn't bothered! She just jumped out of bed and left everything in a tangled, untidy heap!

"How can you sleep in that mess?" asked Milly, her sister.

At lunch time, the rest of the family nibbled their food carefully and always cleaned up after themselves. They brushed up their crumbs and cleared away their bowls. But Molly wasn't bothered! She just munched away merrily, scattering food everywhere!

"Why do you make such a mess?" asked Daddy Mouse.

At playtime, Milly and Max would carefully scamper up cornstalks. But Molly couldn't be bothered! She rushed up the stalks so fast, that she snapped them in two and fell to the ground in a messy heap!

"Why are you so clumsy?" asked Max.

And when Max and Milly collected nuts and seeds for their tea, they always stacked them in neat, little piles. But Molly couldn't be bothered! Her heaps always toppled over.

"Why are you so untidy?" asked Milly.

Everyone was really fed up with Molly and her messy ways.

"Why can't you eat properly?" said Daddy Mouse.

"Why can't you keep yourself clean and tidy?" said Mommy Mouse.

"Why can't you be quieter?" said Baby Mouse.

"Oh, Molly," groaned Milly and Max.

"I can't do anything right," Molly sniffed. "It's not fair." And, with her messy tail in her paw, she said "Good night" and went to bed.

But Molly had a plan. She was fed up with all the grumbling and she wasn't going to put up with it any longer! So, when Max and Milly came to bed, Molly was already fast asleep—at least, that's what they thought. Molly was really wide awake!

She waited until her brother and sister were asleep and then crept out of bed. "No one loves me," she sighed. "I think I'll go and find somewhere else to live." So, off she set!

Molly had no idea where she was going. She scurried along the hedgerow and scampered through the cornstalks. And, as the sun began

to rise, she slipped out of the field and happily skipped down the lane.

"I'll show them!" she said. "Why should I stay at home to be grumbled and moaned at? I'm going to find a home where people want me."

But, as the morning went on and Molly got further and further away from home, she became very tired. She sat down by a farmyard gate. "I'm really sleepy," she said and gave a big yawn! Then Molly noticed the barn door slightly open. Inside was a warm and comfy pile of hay—perfect for a little nap! She snuggled up in the hay and fell fast, fast asleep.

Back at home, when Mommy Mouse came to wake up her little ones, Molly's bed was empty. "Where's Molly?" she asked Milly and Max.

The two little mice rubbed their eyes and looked around.

"We don't know," they said. "She was here last night, fast asleep."

"Daddy! Daddy! Come quick!" called Mommy Mouse. "Our Molly's missing!" So, they searched the house, but Molly was not there. They went outside and looked through the cornfield, combed the hedgerows, searched under and over toadstools, in fact, they didn't leave a leaf unturned! They even went down the lane.

Suddenly, Milly started jumping up and down. "Look!" she squealed, pointing at the muddy path that led into the farmyard.

There, right in front of Milly, was a set of tiny mouse footprints.

Milly and Max followed the footprints across the farmyard and into the barn. And there, fast asleep in a messy pile of hay, was Molly.

"We've found her!" they shouted.

Molly slowly opened her eyes. There were bits of straw sticking to her fur, her whiskers were crumpled, and her paws were muddy. "Oh, Molly!" yelled Milly and Max. "We've missed you so much."

"How can you have missed me?" said Molly. "I'm always such a mess!"

"You might be messy," said her mommy, "but we love you just the same!" Everyone cheered and Molly smiled—they really did love her!

And with that, they set off home.

Night-night Bear

Teddy Bear had been to the circus. "It's very late—why don't you have a nap in the back of the car," said Mommy Bear kindly.

"I'm not sleepy!" said Teddy Bear, stifling a yawn. "Weren't the clowns funny? I want to be a clown when I grow up, I loved the clowns best. And the trapeze artists. I'm going to fly on the trapeze."

"I thought you were going to be a clown," said Daddy Bear, smiling.

"I'll be a clown in my spare time," yawned Teddy Bear.

"What about the trick riders?" asked a smiling Mommy Bear.

"I'll do that as well," sighed Teddy Bear, as his eyes began to close.

All the way home, Teddy Bear dreamed about working in the circus. He made people laugh, and cry, and gasp in amazement at his incredible tricks and jokes.

"Night-night Circus Bear," said Daddy Bear, gently carrying him upstairs to his bed.

"Night-night Daddy," mumbled Teddy Bear through his dreams.

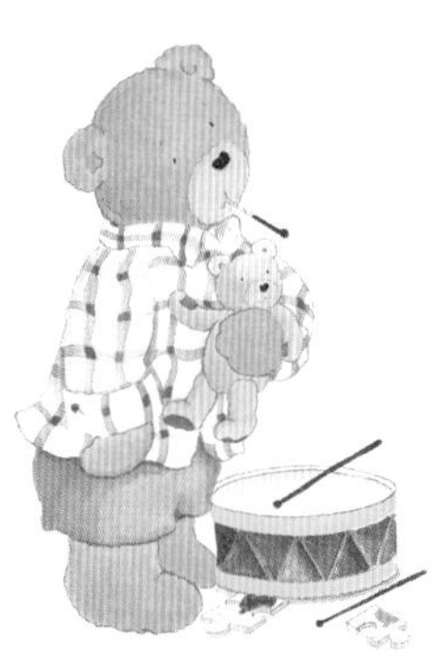

Poorly Bear

Teddy Bear came home from school feeling tired, and poorly. Teddy Bear sat on the sofa and closed his eyes. "I don't want my hot chocolate," he told Mommy Bear. "And I don't want to watch television."

"Do you want to play your drum?" asked Mommy Bear, looking worried. Teddy Bear shook his head, so Mommy Bear went to fetch the thermometer and she put it under Teddy Bear's tongue. "Oh dear," she said. "I'm afraid you're a very poorly Teddy Bear. Up to bed you go!"

The next morning Teddy Bear was covered all over in bright red spots. "You've got chicken pox," said Mommy Bear. "You'll have to stay home from school today."

"Yippee!" said Teddy Bear, but quietly, because his head was sore. Teddy Bear lay on the sofa, watching television and coloring pictures. Mommy Bear read him stories, and gave him soup and ice cream to eat.

After a few days the spots disappeared.

"Can I play my drum?" asked Teddy Bear. Mommy Bear was so glad to see Teddy Bear looking well again, that she let him play his drum for the rest of the afternoon.

Guess What I Want

"Guess what I want," said Ruff to Rufus. "Something from me?" asked Rufus. "Now, let me see—what could it be?"

"You've got to guess," said Ruff.

"You want me to tie a string to the moon, so you can pull it around like a giant balloon?" said Rufus.

"We could tie the moon to the post of your bed, to shine through the night above your head. It would be quite hard to climb up that high, but for you, of course, I'd give it a try," said Rufus.

"Guess again," laughed Ruff.

"You want me to catch you a shining white star, and capture its bright light for you in a jar?" said Rufus.

"It would twinkle all night and light up your dreams, and dance round your room, mixed with yellow moonbeams."

"Would you really fetch me a star?" asked Ruff.

"Well, catching a star isn't easy to do, but I'd give it a try, because I love you," said Rufus.

"Guess again," laughed Ruff.

"You want me to capture the song of the breeze, as it lulls its way gently through leaves on the trees?" said Rufus.

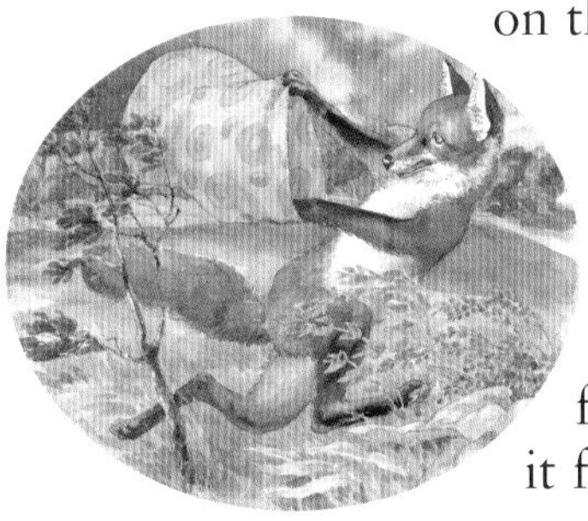

"Would you really bring me the song of the breeze?" asked Ruff.

"Well, the breeze moves so fast, it isn't easy to do, but I'd find a way to do it for you," said Rufus.

Ruff thought hard.

"To tie down the moon, wouldn't be right. And the sky is the place to leave the starlight. It wouldn't be fair to stop the wind's song. Now, try one more guess—your first three were wrong!"

"I know. I was teasing. I think you want this... a huge great big cuddle, and a lovely big kiss!"

Mr. Mole Gets Lost

Mr. Mole poked his little black nose out from the top of one of his molehills and took a great big sniff of the air. Then he sniffed again. And then a third time, just to make sure. "Oh dear," he thought, "it smells like it's going to rain."

Mr. Mole didn't like the rain one bit. Every time he got caught in the rain his plush little velvet fur coat got all wet and drippy, and he left muddy footprints all over his underground burrow. But worse still, the rain got in through the holes in his molehills and then everything got all soggy and took days to dry out.

Well, the skies got darker and darker, and very soon little spots of rain began to fall. Then the spots became bigger. And then bigger still. Before long, all you

could see before your eyes were big, straight rods of rain bouncing off the leaves on the trees, pounding the ground, and turning everything muddy and wet.

Mr. Mole had never seen rain like it. He sat in his burrow in the middle of the meadow, wishing it would stop. But it just kept raining, and raining. Soon the rain started entering his burrow. First it went drip, drip, drip through the holes in his molehills, and then it became a little river of water in the bottom of his burrow. Then the little river became a bigger, faster-flowing river and suddenly Mr. Mole was being washed along by it. Through the tunnels of his burrow he went, this way and then that, as the water gushed and poured through his underground home.

The next thing he knew he was being washed out of his burrow completely as the rain water carried him off down the meadow. Down he went, not knowing which way up he was, or where he was going. Now he was being washed through the woods at the bottom of the meadow, but still the water carried him on, bouncing and turning him until he was dizzy and gasping for breath.

Suddenly, he came to a halt. The rain water gurgled and trickled around him and then flowed onwards, as he found himself stuck firmly in the branches of a bush.

"Oh dear," Mr. Mole said as he got himself free. "Goodness me, where can I be?" he thought. Mr. Mole looked around him, but being a very short-sighted mole—as most moles are—he couldn't make out any of the places that were familiar to him. Worse still, he couldn't smell any smells that were familiar to him. He was completely lost, far from home, and had no idea how to get back again. Now, to make things worse, it was starting to get dark.

"Woo-oo-oo-oo-oo!" said a voice suddenly. Mr. Mole nearly jumped right out of his little moleskin with fright.

"I wouldn't stay here if I were you," said the voice. Mr. Mole looked up and found himself face to face

with a huge owl. "Don't you know it's not safe in the woods at night?" asked the owl. "There are snakes and foxes and weasels and all sorts of nasty creatures that you really wouldn't like to meet."

"Oh dear!" was all Mr. Mole could think of saying. He told the owl of his terrible watery journey, and how he was lost, and didn't know how he was going to get back home again.

"You need to talk to Polly Pigeon," said the owl. "She is a homing pigeon and she lives near your meadow. She can show you the way home. But we'll have to find her first. Stay close to me, mind, and look out for those snakes, foxes and weasels I told you about."

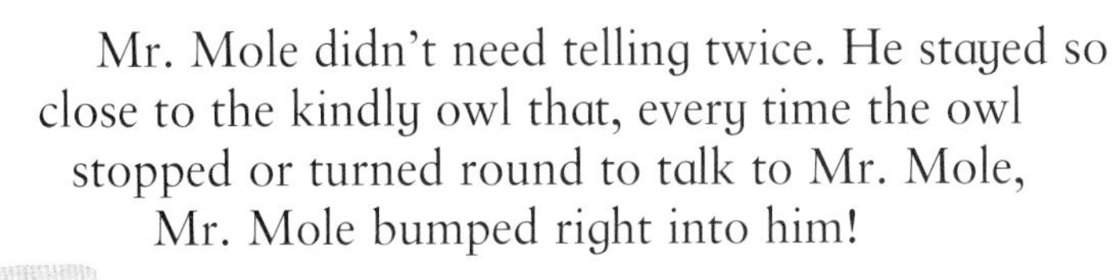

Mr. Mole didn't need telling twice. He stayed so close to the kindly owl that, every time the owl stopped or turned round to talk to Mr. Mole, Mr. Mole bumped right into him!

Through the dark, dangerous woods they went. Every now and again, there would be an unfriendly noise, such as a deep growl or a hiss, coming from the dense, tangled trees, but Mr. Mole didn't want to think about that too much, so he just made sure that he never lost sight of the owl.

Finally, just when Mr. Mole thought that he couldn't go a step further, they came to a halt by an old elm tree.

"Hallo-oooo," called the owl.

They were in luck. Polly Pigeon was waking up, and they found her just in time for she was about to continue her journey home.

"Please," said Mr. Mole, "I'm afraid I'm terribly lost and don't know how to get back to my meadow. Will you take me there?"

"Of course I will," said Polly Pigeon. "We'd better let you rest here a while first, though. But we must go before it gets light."

So Mr. Mole was soon trudging wearily back to his meadow, following as closely behind Polly Pigeon as he was able. Just as the first rays of sun lit the morning sky, Mr. Mole smelled a very familiar smell. It was his meadow! He was almost home!

Soon, he was back in his own burrow. It was so wet and muddy, however, that the first thing he did was build some new tunnels higher up the meadow so that the rain wouldn't wash down into them so easily. Then he settled down to eat one of his supplies of worms, and fell into a deep, well-earned slumber.

Sleepy the Farm Kitten

Sleepy, the farm kitten, was always tired. He loved to sleep all day long, and all through the night. While all the other kittens were busy chasing mice or scaring away birds, he was normally fast asleep.

One day, while the other kittens were chasing mice around the corn shed, Sleepy stretched and looked around for somewhere to nap.

"You can't sleep here," said the farmer's wife, sweeping Sleepy out of the kitchen. "Today's cleaning day and you'll just be in the way."

"You can't sleep here," clucked the hens, flapping him out of the chicken run. "We're laying eggs and we don't want you watching."

"You can't sleep here," mooed the cows, shooing him out of the milking shed. "We're busy being milked, and a kitten can never be trusted around milk."

"I'm really tired," Sleepy complained to a passing mouse. "Can I sleep with you mice?"

"Don't be ridiculous," laughed the mouse. "Don't you know that kittens are supposed to chase mice?"

Just as Sleepy was about to give up hope of ever finding somewhere to sleep, he spotted the ideal bed—a soft bale of hay sitting on a trailer. "Purrfect," he purred, curling into a sleepy ball. Within seconds, he was fast asleep.

He was so comfortable, that he didn't even wake up when the tractor pulling the trailer chugged into life. And he still didn't wake up when the tractor and trailer bumped down the road leading to town. It was only when the trailer shuddered to a halt that Sleepy woke with a start. He blinked his eyes, stretched, and looked around—he was at market and the farmer was driving away in the tractor!

Sleepy started to walk home. He walked all afternoon and through the night. The rooster was crowing when he arrived back at the farm.

"Hello, lazybones," called the other kittens when they saw him. "Where have you been sleeping all night while we chased mice?"

But for once Sleepy really was tired—far too tired to explain where he had been all night. And it wasn't long before he was fast asleep!

Vicky the Very Silly Vet

"Good morning!" calls Vicky Vet as she opens the door to her surgery. "How are all my animals today?"

Vicky starts her early morning rounds with Goldie Goldfish. Vicky Vet loves looking after animals but sometimes she gets very mixed up! She knows she has a busy morning ahead of her, so Vicky wants to get all the cages cleaned, and the animals fed, before her first patient arrives. "I'll give you some clean newspaper first, Patch," she says to the messy puppy, "and then I'll give your blanket a good shake, Tabby."

"There you are, Tabby. A nice fluffy bed for you," says Vicky, putting the blanket back into Tabby's basket, when... Brriiing, brriiing! Brriiing, brriiing! "That's the phone, Tabby," she cries.

Vicky Vet drops everything and rushes to answer it.

"Now, where was I?" thinks Vicky Vet to herself, coming back to the cages.

"I was just about to give you some fresh wood chips, wasn't I?" she says to Hickory and Dickory, the two mice. Just as she is putting the wood chips in the mouse cage...

Ding dong! goes the doorbell. "Who can that be?" Vicky wonders.

"My first patient's not due for half an hour!" Vicky hasn't noticed that the cage doors are open and Patch is busy chasing Tabby around the room!

It is Millie the Mail Carrier with a parcel that is too big to fit through the mailbox. "Thank you, Milly," says Vicky, "but I don't think this parcel is for me. It's addressed to Tony's Pizza Parlor."

"Oh dear!" says Millie. "Why am I so mixed-up? Sorry, Vicky!"

"Now, what next?" asks Vicky Vet, as she finishes cleaning Percy Parrot's cage, but suddenly she feels something scampering up her leg!

"Oh no!" cries Vicky. "Hickory and Dickory, how did you escape? And Patch and Tabby! How did you get out?" Very silly Vicky is flapping about trying to catch all the animals, and all the time Percy is hopping closer to the open door of his cage. First Vicky dives at Tabby and then pounces on Hickory and Dickory and then chases Patch.

Patch is back in his cage when, suddenly, there is a loud squawk! Percy Parrot is flying towards the open window!

"Wait! Percy! Stop!" she cries, rushing after the parrot. Luckily, Vicky catches Percy just in time. Once he is safely back in his cage, she manages to round up Hickory and Dickory, get Tabby back into her basket, and shut Patch safely into his cage.

"Phew!" she puffs. "I feel as if I've done a whole morning's work already. I think after all this, it must be time for some breakfast!"

Vicky lines up the feeding bowls and animal feed on the table. Carefully, she measures out some delicious dog food for Patch and gives him a big juicy bone to chew. Then she spoons out some crunchy bird seed for Percy, some fishy cat food for Tabby, and some tasty sunflower seeds for the mice. Vicky has nearly finished making breakfast for the animals when... Ding dong! It's the doorbell again.

"Oh!" she cries. "My first patient is here already! I'd better hurry!"

So as quickly as she can, Vicky puts the food bowls in the cages—but she doesn't look to see who is getting what! So Patch the dog gets a bowl of crunchy bird seed. Hickory and Dickory the mice get the dog food and the big juicy bone. Tabby the cat gets the tasty sunflower seeds. And Percy the parrot gets the fishy cat food!

What's more, Vicky is in such a rush that she leaves all the cage doors open again!

This time, though, the animals know just what to do. Hickory and Dickory find their sunflower seeds in Tabby's basket. Tabby discovers her fishy cat food in Percy's cage. Percy pecks at his bird seed in Patch's cage. And Patch finds his delicious dog food in the mouse cage.

Fireman Fred is at the door. He has brought his dog Dot for a check-up.

"Do come in," says Vicky Vet. "You are right on time."

"We always like coming here," says Fireman Fred. "The animals are always so happy and everything seems so relaxed.

I'm always so frazzled. What's your secret, Vicky?"

Very silly Vicky thinks about her crazy morning and wonders what dreadful mess will greet Fred as they walk into the surgery. But clever Patch, Tabby, Percy, and Hickory and Dickory are back in their own cages. As Vicky walks in with Fireman Fred and Dot, she sees the clean and tidy room and grins at her animals.

"Treats for tea," she whispers!

The Crazy Professor

Professor Von Bean was very excited. His new machine was ready to use. It was very complicated and he was very proud of it.

The professor called his assistant to come to watch him start the machine. The wheels were green, and brown, and there were levers on either side. The side panels were striped red, and white, and there was a big chimney on the top for the smoke to escape. There was a closet on the side which, the professor explained, was to hang a wet coat. There was a shelf on the back for a box of plants.

While Professor Von Bean was getting more and more excited, his assistant looked very worried and puzzled.

"But what does it do?" he asked, timidly.

The professor scratched his head while he thought of an answer.

"Oh dear, oh dear!" he sighed. "What a fool I have been! Why didn't I think of that? It does absolutely nothing useful at all!"

My Funny Family

I think that there is definitely something very strange about my family, in fact they are all very funny!

My auntie May has got a brain like a sieve, she forgets where things live. She puts a chop in the teapot and carrots in the mugs!

My uncle Fred has ears like cauliflowers, he can hear an ant whistling from a mile away, butterflies beating their wings and woodlice snoring!

My cousin Bob has eyes like a hawk, he can see from New York to London and unknown planets orbiting in space!

My brother Tom has spiders, and bugs up his sleeve, which he loves to wave under my nose so that I scream.

My dog Jasper will eat anything, but especially loves burger and fries, cup cakes, and buttered toast.

Luckily I am not so strange, I just like to dance all day!

Ballerina Belle

Belle the ballerina is a beautiful ballet dancer. She loves to dance in her frilly tutu and satin ballet shoes. She has a best friend—Pearl, a fluffy white kitten with big blue eyes. Pearl enjoys watching Belle dance, spinning, and twirling across the floor.

Today Belle is getting ready for a very special show. The little kitten sits on her friend's pink dressing table purring with delight, as Belle carefully dusts a sprinkling of powder over her face.

Belle is so excited, and nervous. Tonight, she will dance for the King and Queen.

Pearl purrs her approval as the little ballerina puts on a blue tutu that glistens with jewels. Then she ties the pretty ribbons on her shoes.

Finally, Belle puts a gold tiara in her hair. Pearl thinks she looks wonderful. Now Belle is ready for the show and tiptoes to the stage...

The music starts and Belle begins to twirl gracefully across the floor. The King and Queen love to watch her dance—she is the most beautiful ballerina ever.

As the audience cheers, Pearl purrs with delight. Belle's the happiest ballerina in the world.

A Hat Like That

Heather the cow took great care of her appearance. She had the shiniest hooves and the glossiest coat of any of Old MacDonald's cows. She was very proud of having already won three rosettes at the Country Show, and she wanted to win more.

One windy afternoon, when Heather was standing near a hedge, she found a beautiful straw hat on a branch. It had a couple of holes in it, but an elegant cow has to put her ears somewhere!

She strolled back across the field with her nose in the air, and the hat placed firmly on her head. Heather couldn't wait to show it off to her friends.

But to Heather's annoyance, Poppy, Annabel, and Emily simply carried on munching. Heather tried to attract their attention with a tiny ladylike cough, but the munching didn't stop for a second. So Heather coughed a little louder—and the munching grew louder.

Heather couldn't bear it any longer. "Haven't you noticed it?" she mooed.

"Oh! Did I hear someone say something?" asked Emily.

"Yes! It was me!" cried Heather, crossly.

"Oh, so it was," said Annabel, and then she returned to a particularly juicy clump of green grass and carried on chewing.

"I'm feeling rather sleepy after all that lovely grass, I think I'll just have a little snooze," said Poppy.

"And I'm going for a walk," said Emily.

Heather was not a patient cow. "Look at my hat!" she cried. Of course, the other cows had noticed the hat, but they loved to tease their friend.

"I always think," said Poppy, "that hats are rather... old-fashioned."

"What nonsense!" Heather replied, quickly. "Only the most fashionable cows are wearing hats these days." And she gazed at her reflection in a puddle—and thought how lovely she looked in her wonderful hat.

"It's a new hat then, is it?" asked Annabel.

"Certainly!" Heather replied. "I can assure you that this hat is absolutely the very latest style."

And with that, Heather walked around in a circle, moving her head this way and that, so that her friends could admire her hat from every angle. There really was no doubt in Heather's mind that this hat was her crowning glory!

"But don't you remember Mrs MacDonald had a hat just like that a few years ago?" asked Emily.

"I don't think so!" Heather said firmly. "Mrs MacDonald is lovely, but she's not what you would call stylish. Only a prize-winning cow could carry off a hat like this."

"If you say so, dear," mooed Annabel.

And with that, the other cows all went back to munching the juicy grass, while Heather continued to parade around the field.

That evening, the cows ambled into the farmyard to be milked. Before long, all the other animals had gathered round and seemed to be discussing something very funny.

"They're admiring my hat!" whispered Heather to Poppy.

But the giggling and chuckling didn't sound as if they thought Heather looked beautiful. It sounded more like animals who thought she looked rather silly.

"So that's what happened to Scarecrow Sam's hat! I wondered where it had disappeared to," cried Old MacDonald.

Nowadays, if Heather starts putting on airs and graces, Poppy, Emily, and Annabel know just what to do—talk turns to hats, and Heather tiptoes away.

Ebby the Smallest Puppy

Ebby was the smallest puppy in the litter. His brothers and sisters were always teasing him.

"Out of the way, tiny!" they laughed, as they pushed him to the side at meal times.

"You're small because you were the last to be born," explained his mom. "And that's why you're so special." But Ebby didn't feel very special. In fact, he just felt sad.

One day, a family came to see the puppies. "Look smart," said their mother. "They've come to take one of you home."

One of the puppies was chosen, and after that, lots of people came to the house. Each of them left with a puppy of their own, but nobody chose Ebby. Eventually, Ebby was the only puppy left.

"Nobody wants me," sniffed Ebby. "I'm not as good as other dogs."

"Don't be silly," said his mom. "You're just special, you'll see."

The next day, a little girl came to the house. "Oh, goody! They saved him for me," she laughed.

Then, as he was growling at the top of his voice, a funny thing happened. His voice began to crack. He tried to clear his throat, but it was no use. No matter how hard he tried, he could not make a sound. He had lost his voice completely!

"Well it serves you right!" said Rag Doll. "All you do is moan, moan, moan, and we're tired of listening to you. We put the bandage on your mouth to teach you a lesson. But now you've moaned so much that you've made yourself lose your voice completely."

With that, a big tear rolled down Tough Ted's cheek. He was not so tough after all, and he hadn't realized that he moaned so much. He felt very sorry.

Rag Doll did not like seeing Tough Ted so sad.

All the toys felt a bit guilty for what they had done.

"I'll go and get some honey from the kitchen," said Rag Doll. "It will soothe your throat. But you must promise not to start moaning again."

After Rag Doll had given Tough Ted a spoonful of honey, he whispered, "I'm sorry. I promise I'll try not to moan any more. I didn't realize I'd become such a grumpy old bear."

With that, all the toys gave Tough Ted a hug and Rag Doll gave him some more honey.

Since then Tough Ted has tried really hard not to moan. But, whenever he does, he thinks about the bandage and quickly stops himself before anyone hears! And the rest of the toys do their best to look after him, and keep him happy.

Clever Boogie

Boogie was a very clever pig. Most pigs aren't very clever. They can't do math. Every single day they are given pig food to eat, and they say, "Oink! Oink! Pig food! My favorite!" They don't remember it's always the same. But Boogie remembered every horrible meal he'd ever had, and was really fed up with pig food. It tasted like minced garbage!

Boogie lived in his own pen. A horse and a cow lived in the field outside the pigpen and there were trees in the field too. One day, acorns started falling from the biggest tree. The tree was a long way from Boogie, but just a few acorns bounced over and into his pen. An apple from another tree rolled until it rolled into Boogie's pen. So Boogie ate the acorns. Now, acorns are really horrible to eat, but Boogie thought they were delicious! Then he ate the apple. He had never eaten anything so good in his life! He wanted all the acorns, and apples, but he could not reach them. Suddenly, he had an idea.

Next to Boogie's pigpen was an old animal shed that had fallen to pieces. Bricks, and wood were spread about, and wavy metal roof panels lay nearby. Boogie said to the cow and the horse, "Please will you move that metal roof, the barrel, and the drainpipe for me? I'll give you some of my food if you do."

"We have all this grass to eat!" said the cow and the horse.

"But these are delicious lumps of pig food!" replied Boogie.

"Oh, all right!" they said, and they pushed the roof, the barrel, and the drainpipe under the apple tree.

Boogie gave the cow and the horse some of his pig food. They chewed for ages before they realized pig food did not have any actual taste in it, and they spat it out.

When the next apple fell, it rolled down the iron roof into the drainpipe, and flew into Boogie's pen! An acorn bounced off the barrel, and soon there were apples and acorns falling everywhere, and then bouncing straight into Boogie's pen.

Boogie dashed round, catching apples and acorns before they could even touch the ground! And he never had to eat pig food again!

The Birthday Party

Rosy was walking down the stairs when the mail popped through the mailbox and flopped on to the mat. One envelope had a picture of a rabbit and Rosy's name written in big writing on it. She picked it up and rushed into the kitchen. "Look, Mom!" cried Rosy, "a letter for me. Who do you think it's from?"

"I don't know," replied Mom. "Let's open it and find out."

Inside the envelope was an invitation to a party from Rosy's friend, Laura. "Wow! A party!" cried Rosy. "I can't wait!" she said and, with a little bit of help, answered "yes" to the invitation. But then, Rosy began to worry.

"What am I going to buy Laura as a present for her birthday?" she asked.

Mom had an idea. “Let’s go into town tomorrow and look for something special.” So, the next day, Rosy and Mom went to the toy shop. “What does Laura like best?” asked Mom.

“Rabbits,” said Rosy. “Laura loves them.”

“Come with me,” smiled Mom. “I’ve seen just the thing.”

Mom took Rosy to a corner of the toy shop, where they found lots of fluffy toys. And there sat a cute little rabbit, with bright blue pants, and a tiny orange carrot. “Do you think Laura would like that rabbit?” asked Mom.

“She would love him,” said Rosy. So, they bought the rabbit, and some wrapping paper, and went back home.

At home, Rosy wrapped the rabbit in the pretty paper. Then, she drew a card with a big rabbit on the front and wrote her name in red crayon inside it. “Mom,” asked Rosy, “what will I do at the party?”

“Well, there will be lots of games to play,” said Mom.

"I can't wait!" said Rosy.

At last, the afternoon of the party arrived. Rosy put on her pretty party dress. Mom gave her Laura's card and present. "Mom," asked Rosy, "what if I don't like the food?"

"Don't worry," said Mom. "At parties, there are always lots of tasty things to eat—I promise."

"I can't wait!" cried Rosy and skipped out of the door.

When Rosy arrived at the party, Laura opened the front door. There were lots of children standing behind her, but Rosy couldn't see anyone else that she knew.

"Hello, Rosy," said Laura, giving her a big hug. Rosy gave Laura her birthday present. As Laura pulled off the paper, a huge smile spread across her face.

"Oh, Rosy!" she cried. "He's perfect!"

Everyone wanted to hold the rabbit. Rosy felt better already.

"Time for some games!" called Laura's mom. Rosy stood by the door and watched.

"I don't know how to play," she whispered.

"Just do what I do," said Laura and held her friend's hand. Rosy was soon having a wonderful time. Party games were great fun.

Just then, Laura's mom said, "It's time for the birthday tea."

Rosy couldn't wait to see what party food there was to eat. She was feeling really hungry!

"Wow!" gasped Rosy, when she saw the food. All of her favorite things were there—sausages, pizza, cakes, and strawberry jello! There were balloons, paper plates, and cups, which all had rabbits on them.

Rosy sat next to Laura. "Wait till you see my cake," laughed her friend.

At that moment, Laura's mom walked into the room. She was carrying a birthday cake—in the shape of a big rabbit! Laura blew out the candles and everyone sang "Happy birthday!" as loudly as they could.

After tea, everyone played Pass the Parcel. Rosy really liked this game. It was very exciting, waiting for the music to stop and then watching, while someone tore the paper off the parcel. "I can't wait for my turn," thought Rosy. Suddenly, the music did stop, just as Rosy held the parcel. And this time, there was only one piece of paper left. She ripped it off—inside was a jigsaw puzzle.

It wasn't long before moms and dads came to take their children home. "Thanks for my rabbit," said Laura, to Rosy.

"And thanks for a great party," said Rosy.

Then, Laura gave everyone a balloon and a badge—with a rabbit on it. On the way home, Mom asked Rosy if she'd had a good time.

"Oh, yes!" said Rosy. "The games were fun, Laura's other friends were great and the food was really yummy! Mom," asked Rosy, "how long is it until my birthday?"

"It's about four weeks," said Mom. "Why?"

"Please may I have a birthday party?" replied Rosy. "I've got lots of friends to invite and I know just which games I want to play. And I'd really like a big dinosaur cake."

"I can't wait!" laughed Mom.

Desmond Grows Up

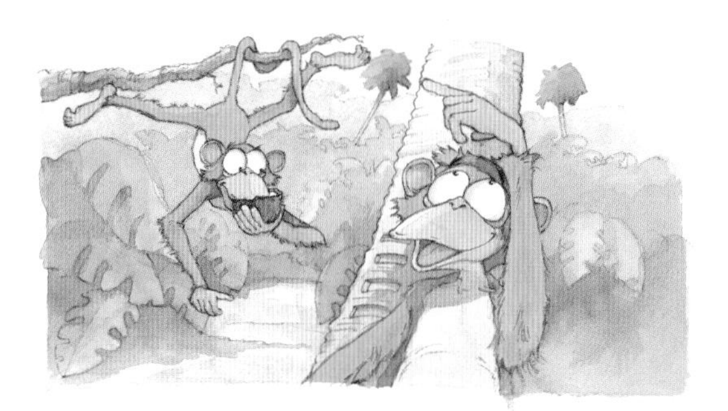

Desmond was the smallest monkey in the group. He couldn't wait to grow up. "Will you measure me?" he asked his friend Rodney. "I only measured you last Monday, and now it's Friday," said Rodney. "You won't have grown in four days!"

Rodney took him to the tallest tree in the jungle and made him stand with his back against it. Then he made a mark on the trunk level with the top of Desmond's head. It was in the same place as the last mark.

Later Desmond spoke to his friend Bubbles. "Watch the top of my head," he said to her.

"Whatever for, Dethmond?" said Bubbles. She always called him Dethmond.

"Am I growing? Look at the top of my head. Can you see me growing?" asked Desmond.

"No, of course not!" she said. "I knew it!" said Desmond. "I knew it! I'm never going to grow."

One day, there was a competition to see who could collect the most coconuts from the tall palm trees. Rodney was the favorite to win. He climbed to the top and wriggled through the palm leaves, and then... he got stuck!

"Help!" he cried. "I can't move."

One of the big monkeys went up to help, but he was too big to get through the leaves.

"Let me try," begged Desmond.

"OK," they said grudgingly. Desmond raced up the trunk. At the top he was small enough to reach his friend and help him to get free. Then he picked six or seven coconuts and dropped them to the ground.

When they climbed down, the other monkeys crowded round to pat Desmond on the back.

"Wow!" said Bubbles. "No one has ever climbed a palm tree as fast as that before."

"Maybe you are all too big!" said Desmond happily. "I'm not in such a hurry to grow up after all!"

After that he didn't worry so much about being small, especially after he managed to collect more coconuts than anyone else, and won the competition!

A Good Example

Tilly and Old George were kind old horses, but they didn't understand the young animals who tore around the farmyard.

"Look at that piglet," Tilly grumbled, loudly, one day. "Look! He's leaving lots of muddy trotter-prints all over the yard."

"And those noisy chicks and ducklings are not behaving very well either," neighed Old George, nodding his head in agreement. "They should know better than to cheep and quack during our afternoon nap."

"Things were very different in the old days," sighed Tilly. "Youngsters were well brought up then. When we were foals, we were tidy and very, very quiet."

Unfortunately, Tilly and Old George didn't keep their feelings to themselves…

The next morning, Tilly told Percy the pig how to discipline his piglets. Old George gave Jenny and Henrietta the hens some advice and tips on bringing up chicks. And both the horses had a word with Doris the duck about the correct time and place for ducklings to quack.

By lunch time, there wasn't a single animal in the farmyard who wasn't feeling cross with Tilly and Old George.

"Huh! I'd like to see them look after even one little one," complained Doris.

Strangely enough, it was that afternoon that Old MacDonald brought a new foal to the farm for Tilly and Old George to care for. Percy, Jenny, Henrietta and Doris looked forward to having some fun!

But the animals were disappointed. The new foal, whose name was Frances, was remarkably good. She never spilled her oats, or splashed the water in her trough. She wasn't noisy, or nosy, or naughty.

Worse still, Tilly and Old George looked terribly pleased with themselves.

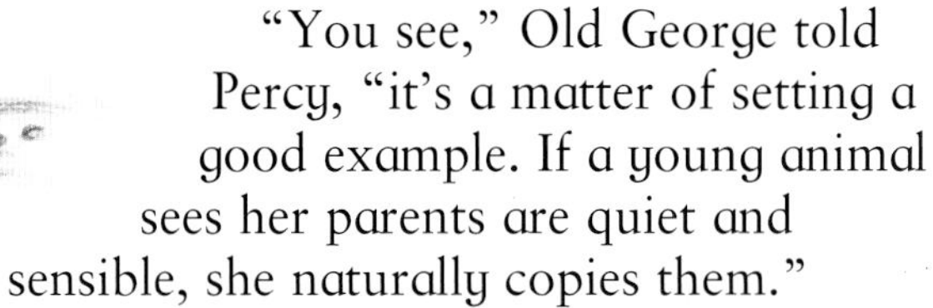

"You see," Old George told Percy, "it's a matter of setting a good example. If a young animal sees her parents are quiet and sensible, she naturally copies them."

As Old George was talking, he made a big, sweeping gesture with his left hoof, and his shoe, which had been a little loose lately, flew right off!

The shoe shot right across the farmyard. With a loud clang! it knocked over a pail of pig food. Then with a clonk! it bounced straight off the pail and whizzed right through a window and into the farmhouse kitchen with a huge crash! of broken glass.

Mrs. MacDonald stormed out into the yard. She was looking extremely angry. The animals waited...

In her hand was a hot apple pie with a large horseshoe sticking in it!

"Who has done this," she cried, "and made so much noise and mess?"

Old George tried to look unconcerned and calm, but the eyes of every other animal in the farmyard were upon him. Who else had shoes that big? There was no way that Old George could talk his way out of this!

These days, Tilly and Old George are not quite so quick to criticize their friends. And when the nights are cold, and everyone needs cheering up, the story of George's flying footwear still brings a smile to everyone's face—all except for Mrs. MacDonald, of course!

Mermaid Marina

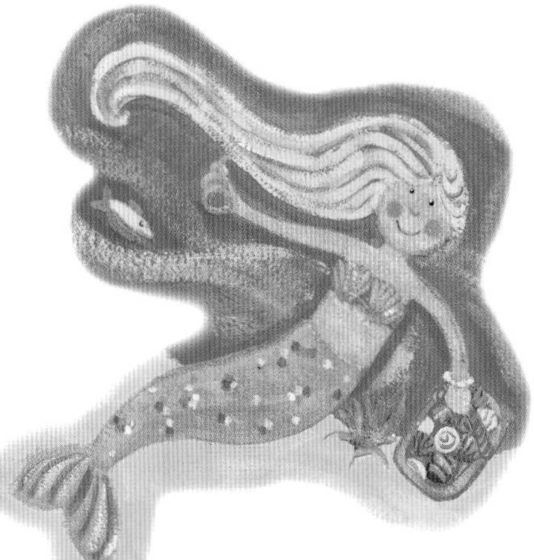

In a magical cave, down at the bottom of the deep blue sea, lives Marina, a beautiful mermaid with a shimmering tail. She glides through the water, searching for shiny pearls and sparkling shells.

Coral the dolphin is Marina's very best friend. They love to twirl and dive through the crystal blue waters, and play hide-and-seek amongst the colorful seaweed.

Today there is great excitement at the bottom of the sea. It's the Sea King's birthday and there will be a grand party.

Marina is getting ready. She puts on a pretty necklace made from glistening pearls, a beautiful shell bracelet, and some tiny starfish earrings.

"How do I look, Coral?" she asks her friend. Coral flaps her fins and does a special dolphin twirl—Marina looks wonderful! Finally, the mermaid brushes her beautiful long hair and weaves some tiny blue sea-flowers into it. Then, with a flick of their tails, Marina and Coral head off for the party.

When they arrive at the palace, the other mermaids are amazed—Marina looks so pretty!

"Happy Birthday, Your Majesty!" she says, and gives the king her present—a precious pearl.

"Thank you, Marina," says the king, "it's almost as lovely as you are."

Ode to Ghosts

You may not know this, but the life of a castle ghost is very sad. He spends his days haunting cold, lonely rooms and corridors, and he never gets invited to parties. All day long the ghost floats from one room to another. He howls, and clanks his chains, but most people blame the noise on the wind outside or the ancient drains. Occasionally he might appear when everyone is sitting eating their supper, in the hope of a snack and a chat, but everyone screams, and runs away. Naturally this doesn't make him feel any better.

What is even worse, the poor ghost has to wander around all night while everyone else is tucked up in bed! He would really like a warm bed to sleep in—but as soon as anyone wakes up they scream, and shout so loudly that the ghost feels embarrassed and slips away.

So, the next time you see a ghost wafting along a castle corridor, don't run away in fright. Stay a while, and have a chat, you'll find him most polite!

The Queen of the Monsters

Towards the end of the year all the monsters met in a huge cave to vote for their new queen. The tales of their misbehavior made the headlines in the newspapers, but Mog decided she would see for herself.

As she arrived, Mog heard Trundle the Troll let out one of his infamous roars in the depths of the cave. The sound was so loud that it knocked her over! As she picked herself up Hagar the Hairy, who was terribly scary, strode past, leaving a trail of disgusting dribble. Slod the Slimeball was the favorite to win—she was a disgrace, even for a monster! But the monsters all crowded round little Mog. They were fascinated by her, she was so small and sweet. She had four dainty feet and a charming smile—not very monstrous at all!

After the vote, the noise was appalling as the monsters discussed who should win, and Mog felt sure that Slod the Slimeball would be the new queen. So she was amazed when it was announced that she was to be the new queen! For once the monsters had decided that they didn't want a queen they would dread —so they voted for little Mog instead!

Cuddly's Sweater

Cuddly Sheep and Stout Pig were going to show the others how to knit. Cuddly Sheep was really good at knitting, but she needed Stout Pig to help with the wool. Stout Pig couldn't knit, but he was very good at spinning wool. He collected all the loose bits of wool that caught on thorny bushes around the farm and made long, beautiful lengths of yarn out of them. Then Cuddly used Stout Pig's yarn to knit lots of pretty things. She could knit the best wooly sweaters in the world!

Stout Pig sat with his back against a low hedge and Cuddly sat on the other side. The pig pulled out lengths of wool from a pile under the hedge. He started to spin the wool on his wheel, until it was twisted into yarn. Then he gave the end to Cuddly.

Cuddly made little loops of the wool and put them on two fat knitting needles. Then she started knitting.

"Knit one, purl one, knit two together," she whispered to herself. Only knitters know what these secret words mean. They must be magic words, because they are whispered over and over again.

Stout had to work hard to keep up with Cuddly Sheep.

Cuddly looked up. "Is it getting late? I'm getting a bit cold," she said. None of the others felt cold.

"You can put my blanket on," said Pebbles Horse. He pulled his blanket over Cuddly's shoulders. But Cuddly got colder. And colder!

"I keep warm in the straw," said Saffron Cow. She covered Cuddly with straw. But the more Cuddly knitted, the colder she got.

And the hotter Stout became. Cuddly was trying to finish the sweater quickly before she froze. The faster she knitted, the faster Stout Pig had to turn the spinning wheel, and he was soon in a sweat!

Then the sweater was finished... and Cuddly was shivering! Her teeth were chattering! Pebbles looked hard at Stout. Then Pebbles' large head followed the wool from the spinning wheel over the hedge. "Cuddly," said Pebbles, "I think you have been knitting your own wool!"

As Cuddly jumped up in surprise the blanket and the straw fell off. She was bare all around her middle. No wonder she was cold. Her wool was all gone.

"Oh well," said Cuddly Sheep, taking out the needles from her knitting. "Never mind! I have a nice thick new sweater to keep me warm!"

Benny the Barmy Builder

Benny was a hard-working builder, and he always did his very best. But sometimes he could be forgetful!

One morning, Benny the Builder arrived bright and early at Vicky Vet's surgery. "Benny the Builder at your service!" he announced. "I think you have a job for me to do."

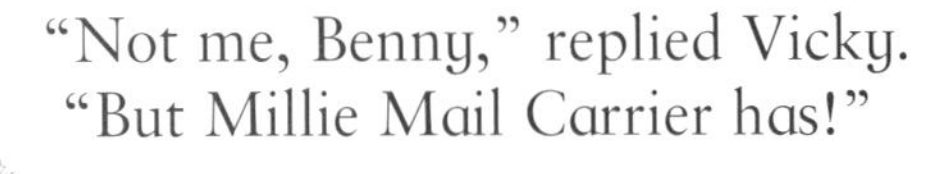

"Not me, Benny," replied Vicky. "But Millie Mail Carrier has!"

"Of course!" said Benny. "Sorry—I really shouldn't be so forgetful!"

And off he went to Millie Mail Carrier's house. "Benny the Builder at your service!" Benny announced. "Woof!" said Benny's dog, Rocky.

"Come in," called Milly, and she took out a drawing to show Benny.

"I would like you to build a playhouse in my yard," Millie said. "It's a surprise for my grandchildren, Peter, Penny, and Patty. I did this drawing to show you just how it should look."

Benny and Millie looked at the drawing together.

"The playhouse should have two tall doors," said Millie, "one at the front and one at the back, with one small step at the back door. There should be five windows, one at either side of the front door and one on each of the other sides."

"Yes, I see," said Benny.

"And I want a nice sloping roof," said Millie, "not a flat roof!"

"I will do my best!" said Benny.

Millie left for the post office, and Benny went out to start work. But he had barely begun when a gust of wind came along.

WHOOSH! went Millie's drawing, up in the air.

"WOOF!" barked Rocky, leaping up to catch it.

Oh no! The drawing got caught in the branches of a tree!

Rocky managed to fetch the drawing but, by the time Benny got it back, it was in shreds.

"Oh dear!" moaned Benny the Builder. "How will I build the playhouse now?"

Benny tried to remember everything in the drawing. But he quickly got very confused!

"Was it five windows, and two doors with one step?" Benny puzzled. "Or was it two windows, and five doors with three steps? Was the roof flat, and not sloping? Or sloping, and not flat? Were the doors tall or small? Oh dear, oh dear!"

Eventually Benny decided that he would just have to do his best. So, he got to work measuring... mixing... laying bricks... sawing wood... hammering nails... fixing screws... plastering, and painting... and doing his best to make sure it was all just right.

Late that afternoon, Millie Mail Carrier got home from work. She couldn't wait to see what Benny had done. But, what a surprise she had when she saw it! The playhouse's roof was flat. The bottom of the house was sloping. There were two steps leading up to two doors on one side of the house and there were two floors, both different sizes. And there were two windows on one side of the house.

"Oh no! It's all wrong!" said Millie to Benny. "How will you ever fix it in time?"

But Benny didn't have a chance to answer because, just at that moment, Millie's grandchildren arrived.

"Oooh! Look! A playhouse!" they cried happily as they rushed towards it. "There's a door for each of us!" they all cried together.

"And we can climb right up to the roof!" said Patty.

"And slide down the other side!" said Peter.

"And there are loads of windows which makes it nice and bright inside!" said Penny.

"Granny, it's the best playhouse ever!" the children told Millie. "It is perfect. Thank you so much!"

"Well, I think you should thank Benny the Builder," said Millie Mail Carrier, smiling.

Benny the Builder smiled too. "I just did my very best," he said.

Elsie Elephant's Jungle Shower

Up above the jungle there wasn't a cloud in the sky. Deep in the jungle Elsie Elephant was feeling very hot.

"It's even hot in the shade," she grumbled. "I think I'll go to the river to cool off!"

Tommy Monkey was swinging high up in the tree-tops. "I'm going swimming," Elsie told him. "You can come too, if you like." Tommy jumped out of the tree and skipped along with Elsie.

"You've got a very long trunk," said Tommy Monkey. "What is it for?"

Elsie thought about it for a minute. "I'm not really sure," she said at last.

At the river they found Leo Lion standing at the edge of the water, looking in.

"Hello Leo—are you coming for a swim?" asked Elsie.

"Lions don't like swimming," sighed Leo. "But I'm so hot! I'll come and watch you."

Soon Stripy Tiger arrived. She and Leo watched as Elsie and Tommy Monkey dived into the river, and began splashing around in the water.

"It's lovely and cold—jump in!" shouted Elsie.

"Tigers are a bit scared of water," called Stripy. "But it does look fun!"

Elsie saw how hot all her friends looked, and had an idea. She filled her trunk with cool water, and sprayed it all over Leo Lion and Stripy Tiger. Soon Tommy Monkey, and even the jungle birds came to play under Elsie's shower.

"Hooray! Now I know exactly what my long trunk is for!" said Elsie happily, and all the animals cheered!

The Naughty Bears

One sunny summer's day, Ben and Fraser's parents told them to pack their things, as they were going to the beach.

"Yippee!" said Ben. "Can we take our teddies?"

"As long as you keep an eye on them," said Daddy. "We don't want to spend all afternoon looking everywhere for them if you lose them again!"

Ben and Fraser took their teddies everywhere they went, but they were always losing them, and then there was a great hunt to find them. But the truth was, that when no one was looking, the naughty little teddies would run away in search of excitement and adventure.

Today was no different. The family unpacked their things when they arrived at the beach. Mommy read a book and Daddy read a newspaper.

Soon Ben and Fraser were busy building sand castles. When the naughty teddies saw that no one was looking, they jumped up, and ran away giggling, all along the beach.

"Let's go exploring," said Billy, who was the oldest bear. "I can see a cave over there, come on, let's go!" He pointed to a dark hole in the rocks close to the water.

"It looks a bit dark, and scary," said Bella.

"Don't be silly," said Billy. "You're a bear, aren't you? I thought that bears liked dark caves!"

The little bears clambered over the rocks and into the cave. It was very deep, and very dark. Just then, Bella spotted something gleaming on the floor. She picked it up and showed it to Billy.

"Gold!" said Billy, in excitement, taking the little coin from Bella. "This must be a smugglers' cave! Maybe the smugglers are still here. Let's take a look!"

"No!" said Bella. "They could be dangerous. Let's go back." She turned and ran back outside, where she saw to her horror that while they had been exploring the tide had come in, and cut the rocks off from the beach.

"Billy!" she called. "Come quickly, we're stranded!"

Meanwhile, Ben and Fraser had finished making sand castles, and found that their teddy bears were missing.

"Oh, no," groaned Daddy. "Not again!"

The family hunted high and low along the beach, but there was no sign of the bears to be found. "Maybe they've been washed out to sea," said Fraser, his voice trembling at the thought.

Back at the cave the naughty teddies could see their owners looking for them. They jumped up and down, and waved their paws. "It's no use," said Bella, "they can't see us. We're too small."

"Don't worry," said Billy, trying to sound a lot braver than he felt.

Just then, two men appeared from the other side of the rocks. The teddies froze—these must be the smugglers! They trembled in fear as the men picked them up, clambered over the rocks, and tossed them into a little boat that had been hidden from view behind the rocks. The teddies clung together at the bottom of the boat as the men jumped in and began to row. Where were they taking them?

"Oh, Billy, I'm so frightened," whispered Bella. "Do you think they are going to hurt us?"

"No, Bella, I'm sure we'll be fine," answered Billy.

But inside he didn't feel so sure. He was really very worried that they would never get home, or see Ben and Fraser again.

Bella started to cry in little muffled whimpers, and big tears rolled down her cheeks. "If we ever get back home, I'm never going to run away again," she sobbed.

"There, there," comforted Billy, patting her gently.

After a while, the boat stopped, and the men jumped out. They grabbed the bears, and held them in the air high above their heads. One of the men called out in a loud voice, "Has anyone lost these bears?"

Everyone on the beach looked up, and Ben and Fraser raced over and grabbed their bears.

Daddy came running over to join them. He and the boys thanked the men for bringing the bears back. "We've been looking everywhere for them," said Ben and Fraser, grinning with relief.

"We found them up by that cave," said one of the men, pointing over to the cave. "You kids must have left them there."

"But the boys have been here building sand castles all afternoon... " said Daddy, looking puzzled.

No one ever did find out how the naughty teddies got to the cave, or where the little coin in Billy's pocket came from. But from then on the naughty teddies became very good teddies, and they never dared to run away again!

Sparky the Baby Dragon

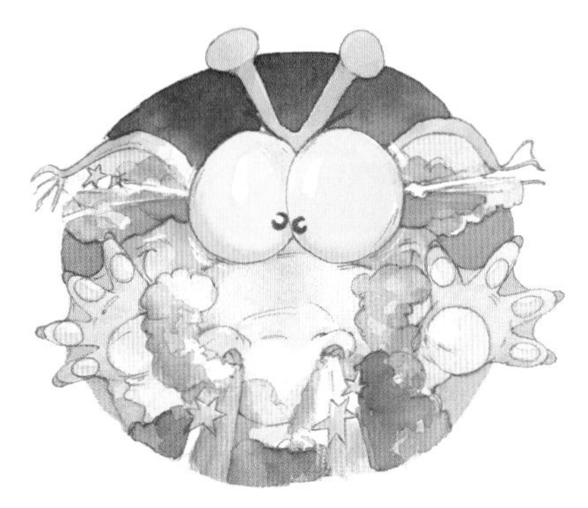

Sparky was a young dragon who lived in a cave far away. Now, as you know, dragons can breathe flames out of their noses! But did you know that baby dragons have to learn how to do it? Sparky watched his mom and dad carefully when they breathed flames, and practiced daily.

One day Mom and Dad had to go out. They told Sparky to stay indoors because there was a wicked witch who hated little dragons, and turned them into teapots just for fun. But Sparky didn't mind staying in. He had some new toy knight figures to play with. He had just started when he heard a bell outside. "Ting-a-ling," it went, "ting-a-ling." And then a voice said, "Ice cream! Ice cream! Come and get your ice cream!"

Sparky peeped out. Outside was a brightly painted ice cream cart and sitting behind the wheel was an old woman with a big grin. Then the woman laughed! It was a loud, cackling laugh, and when Sparky heard it, he knew it was the witch. He slammed the door, and locked it.

"Phew!" thought Sparky. "That was close." The afternoon passed peacefully.

Then, the doorbell rang. "Who is it?" Sparky asked.

"It's Uncle Jack," said a voice, "I've come to take you fishing." Sparky liked fishing with Uncle Jack!

"Is it really you?" he asked. "Of course it is," replied Uncle Jack. He opened the door, and then...

"Got you!" snapped Uncle Jack—and turned into the witch! Sparky gasped. The witch raised her wand, shouted the magic words "Ta-ra-ra-boom-de-ay" and started to spin very fast.

Sparky puffed as hard as he could. Then he had a big surprise! The witch was surrounded by a puff of smoke. And, as the smoke cleared, he saw that she had turned into a teapot!

Just then Mom and Dad came back. "Have you had any trouble while we've been out?" asked Mom.

"Not much!" said Sparky. "But, the next time you go out, please may I come with you?"

"Of course you can!" said Mom. "Now why don't I make some tea in this nice new teapot!"

Granny Casts a Spell

Susie was very fond of her Granny. Each day, when Susie got home from school, Granny was always there, sitting by the fire, knitting. Granny knitted so fast that sometimes it seemed as though the knitting needles sparked in the firelight.

"Do you know," Granny would say, "that I'm really a witch?" Susie always laughed when Granny said that because she didn't look at all like a witch. She had a smiling face, and kind eyes, and she never wore black. Not ever. When Granny wasn't looking, Susie would take a peek inside her closet just in case she might find a broomstick or a witch's hat. But she never found so much as a book of spells.

"I don't believe you're a witch," said Susie.

"I am," replied Granny, "and I'll cast a spell one day. You'll know when that day comes, for my needles will start to knit by themselves."

After that, Susie kept a careful watch over Granny's needles, but they always lay quite still in the basket of knitting.

One day, Susie was playing in her yard when she heard the sound of weeping. The sound seemed to be coming from under the old tree in the corner. She walked towards the tree and as she did so the crying noise got louder, but she could not see anyone there. Then she looked down at her feet, and there—sitting on a mossy stone—was a tiny little man. He was neatly dressed in a yellow velvet vest and knickers. On his feet were beautiful, shiny, buckled shoes, and a three-cornered hat with a wren's feather in it trembled on his shaking head. When the little man saw Susie, he stopped crying and started to dab his eyes with a fine lace handkerchief.

"Whatever can the matter be?" asked Susie, crouching down.

"Oh dear, oh dear!" sobbed the little man. "I am the fairy princess's tailor and she has asked me to make her a lovely gown to wear to the May Ball tonight. But a wicked elf has played a nasty trick on me and turned all my beautiful, fine gossamer fabric into leathery bats' wings.

Now I shall never be able to make the princess's gown and she will be very angry with me."

And he started to cry again.

"Please don't cry!" said Susie. "I'm sure I can help. My Granny's got a sewing basket full of odds and ends. I'll see if she's got anything nice for a party dress. I'm sure she won't mind sparing some—after all, you won't need much," she said. At that, the little man looked a bit more cheerful.

"Wait here," said Susie, "while I run indoors and have a look." She ran up the path, and in through the back door.

"Granny, Granny!" she called. She ran into the sitting room expecting to find Granny knitting by the fire. But Granny had her eyes closed, and she was whispering to herself. On her lap was her knitting—and the needles were moving all by themselves, so that the yarn danced up and down on the old lady's knees.

At first Susie was too astounded to move. Then she thought, "I hope Granny's not casting a bad spell. I must see if the little tailor is all right."

She ran back down the path and there sat the tailor, surrounded by a great pile of gorgeous gossamer, shining in the sunlight.

"I've never seen such fine material—ever!" he exclaimed. "But where did it come from? I just closed my eyes to dab them with my handkerchief, and when I opened them again—there it was!"

"I don't know," said Susie, "but I think my Granny might have had something to do with it."

"Well, I'd never be able to thank her enough," said the tailor. "I shall be able to make the finest gown in the whole of fairyland. The princess will dance all night in the prettiest dress there ever was. I'm also indebted to you, for it was you who helped me in the first place. I would like it very much if you came to the May Ball, too."

"Why, thank you so much," Susie replied, "I should like that very much." She didn't want to hurt the tailor's feelings but she knew she couldn't go—she was far too big to go to a fairy ball!

"Well, I must get on with the dress now," said the little man, reaching for a pair of fairy scissors. "See you tonight!" And with that he vanished.

That night, Susie wondered if the fairies really were having a ball. How she longed to be there! Once she thought she heard a tapping at the window. She sat up in bed, and peered out of the window. Was that the fairy tailor she saw through the glass—or was she imagining it? Then, in the middle of the night, she awoke with a start. There was a click, clicking noise at the end of her bed.

"Granny is that you?" asked Susie.

"Yes, dear," replied Granny. "I couldn't sleep, so I decided to do some knitting. All at once the needles started twitching, so I knew it was time to cast a spell. What is your wish, Susie?"

"I… I… " stammered Susie, "I want to go to the May Ball," she blurted.

"Then you shall go to the Ball, my dear," said Granny.

In an instant, Susie felt herself shrinking. When she looked down she saw she was wearing a beautiful gown, and tiny satin slippers. Then she floated on gossamer wings out through the window, and off to the Ball!

The next morning, Susie woke up in her bed. Had it all been a dream—the revelry, the fairy food, the frog band, and the dance with the handsome fairy prince? Then she saw something peeping out from under her pillow. And what do you think it was? It was a tiny, tiny shred of the finest gossamer fabric.

The Mermaid Fair

Jason loved diving, and he was very good at it. He loved to look for pearls. They are jewels of the sea, and he collected even the tiniest pearl.

One day Jason was diving when he saw a sign on a rock. He was very surprised to read the words: MERMAID FAIR TODAY! Jason had heard of mermaids, of course, but he'd never seen one!

Jason took a huge gulp of air, and swam towards the fair. There was a crowd of mermaids, some were riding dolphins, some were swimming in races, and some were playing games at the stalls. And there were pearls! Two of the mermaids noticed Jason watching and came over to him.

"You're a strange sort of fish!" teased the fair-haired mermaid.

"Hello," said Jason. To his amazement, Jason found he could talk and breathe under water! "Can I go to your fair? I'd love to win some pearls!"

"Oh, pearls are boring," said the other mermaid. "What you want is one of these," and she showed Jason

a plastic comb with a flower on it. She had found it in a rock pool, and thought it was the most beautiful thing she'd ever seen. Jason told her he would bring her many combs if she would show him how to win a pearl.

"That's easy!" she told him. "You just have to win the dolphin race!" But the dolphin race wasn't easy—unless, of course, you are a mermaid! It was nearly time to go, and Jason had not won a single prize! At the very last stall there was a pearl as big as a coconut. He had to throw a sponge at the pearl to knock it over. The mermaids gathered round to cheer him on. He had one or two near misses, and then, amidst lots of laughter, he knocked the huge pearl off the stand with his third try.

"You've won!" the mermaids shouted excitedly. "The pearl is yours!"

Jason swam back to his boat, delighted. The next day he returned clutching a box filled with pretty plastic combs. When the mermaids saw them they danced for joy in the waves, and kissed him on both cheeks.

After that Jason saw the mermaids whenever he went diving, and he always took them a special plastic comb.

I Wish...

I wonder what you would be if you weren't you. I like to sit and think of all the things I would like to be...

Sometimes I wish I was an elephant because I would laugh when I had a bath, and used my nose as a hose to rinse off all my bubbles.

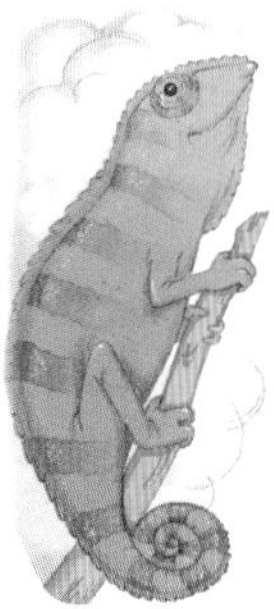

Or I wish I was a chameleon because then I could change the color of my skin to hide anywhere, and no one would be able to see me!

Or if I could be a dolphin I would be able to leap and splash about in the water having fun all day, and swim with the fish.

If I was a hippo I would be able to mess about all day, and get as dirty as I liked, and no one would tell me off.

I think that I will stay as me—but I won't stop wondering about being something else!

A Whale of a Time

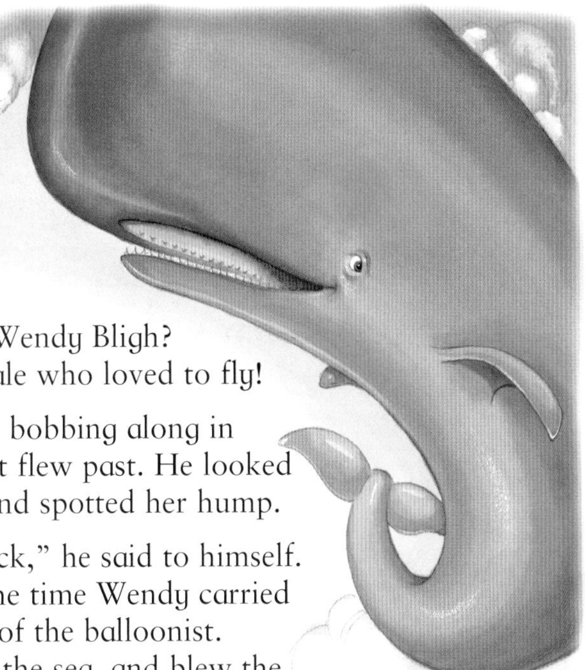

Have you heard the story of Wendy Bligh?
She was a remarkable whale who loved to fly!

One day Wendy was sleeping, bobbing along in the sea, when a hot-air balloonist flew past. He looked down from his balloon basket, and spotted her hump.

"I think I will land on that rock," he said to himself. He tied up his balloon, and all the time Wendy carried on sleeping completely unaware of the balloonist. But then a tornado whirled over the sea, and blew the balloon and Wendy upwards as high as can be.

"What a wonderful feeling," cried Wendy in glee. "I am floating above the sparkling blue sea."

The hot-air balloonist took her for a spin, then dropped her back in the sea at the end of the day.

"Oh thank you!" smiled Wendy, and swam away.

Jade and the Jewels

Jade was the prettiest mermaid in the lagoon! Her long jet black hair reached right down to the tip of her swishy, fishy tail. Her eyes were as green as emeralds, and her skin was as white as the whitest pearl. But Jade was so big-headed and vain that the other mermaids didn't like her!

There *was* someone who was fond of Jade. Gentle the giant turtle followed her everywhere, but Jade didn't notice. She lived in her own world, spending all her time combing her hair, and looking in the mirror.

One day Jade overheard the mermaids talking about a pirate ship that had sunk to the bottom of the ocean. On board was a treasure chest filled with precious jewels. "But no one dares take the jewels," whispered the mermaids, "because the pirate ship is cursed!"

"I'm going to find that pirate ship," Jade told Gentle, "and the treasure chest! Just imagine how beautiful I will look wearing all those jewels!" And Jade set off right away.

"Wait for me," called Gentle, paddling after her.

They swam to a deep part of the ocean they had never been to before. They dove deep down to the very bottom of the ocean. Finally, they found the shipwreck.

"Be careful, Jade," said Gentle. "Remember there is a curse on this pirate wreck."

"Nonsense," Jade replied. "I've come for the jewels! I won't go home without them!" When they found the chest, the lid sprang up, and brilliant jewels spilled out. Jade lifted out a necklace and put it round her neck. She looked even lovelier.

Suddenly, there was a loud crack, and the necklace turned to stone—it was the ship's curse! Jade tried to swim, but the necklace was so heavy she couldn't move.

"Help!" Jade cried out. "Help! Help!" Gentle swam over, and his powerful flippers broke the necklace to free Jade.

As they swam away from the wreck, Gentle said, "You don't need fancy jewels, Jade. You're very pretty without them."

Once she was safely home, Jade told the other mermaids about the pirate ship curse.

"I've learned my lesson," said Jade. "I'll never be vain again."

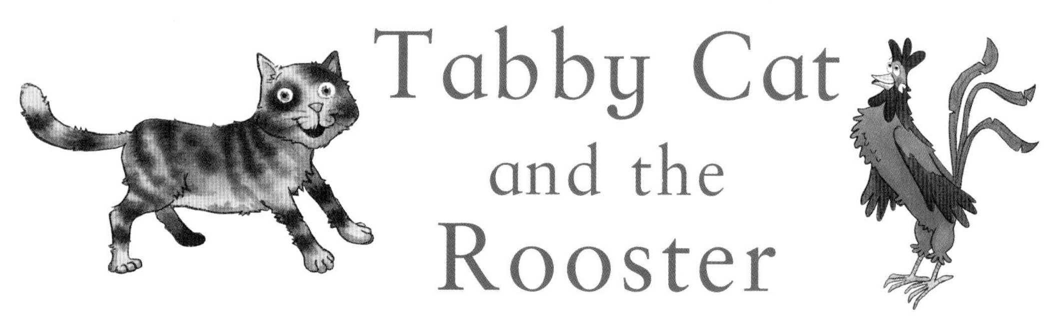

Tabby Cat and the Rooster

Haven Farm is not only a hospital. There are also lots of animals, who live on the farm all the time. One of these is Tabby the cat. She came as a stray kitten, a long time ago. Sally and Joe fell in love with her straight away, and Tabby soon became part of the family. Tabby likes nothing better than to curl up in a sunny, quiet corner of the barn. But there is one thing that spoils Tabby's peace and quiet—Charlie the rooster.

"Poor Tabby," said Sally one day, as she stroked the cat's head. "She just doesn't like Charlie."

"Well, he is noisy, and bossy," said Joe. Charlie was strutting along the gate, watching Tabby out of the corner of his eye.

"Cock-a-doodle-doo!" he crowed, loudly. Suddenly, Tabby jumped out of Sally's arms and ran towards the rooster.

"No, Tabby, no!" shouted Sally. But, as Tabby leapt up at the cheeky rooster, Charlie just fluttered into the safety of the henhouse, clucking and squawking. This was a game that Tabby and Charlie had played many times before.

"Missed him again!" laughed Joe. Tabby just looked cross, and walked off to the barn for some peace and quiet.

A few days later, Tabby wasn't really in the mood for Charlie's antics. Her ear was hurting and, every time Charlie crowed, it made her feel worse. So, she curled up in her favorite spot, and tried to go to sleep. "Cock-a-doodle-doo!" cried Charlie, suddenly. Tabby screeched, and fled across the farmyard. Charlie thought how clever he had been to scare Tabby, and crowed loudly again.

"Hey Sally, look at Tabby!" cried Joe. Sally looked up to see Tabby running across the yard, as fast as she could go.

"Something's frightened her," said Joe.

Then, they saw Charlie, looking very pleased with himself. They knew that he had been up to his old tricks again!

"Come on, Joe," said Sally. "We must find Tabby." They walked towards the cowshed, where they had last seen her.

"Look!" said Joe. "There she goes." As they watched, Tabby ran straight up the side of the cowshed, and jumped on to the roof.

"Oh, no!" said Sally. "We'll never get her now." At last, Tabby stopped running. That silly rooster had really frightened her. Tabby looked around. The ground looked a long way down! She took a few, careful steps, but suddenly she felt very dizzy, and started to fall. Tabby landed with a bump! She had slipped off the roof, and was now stuck between the cowshed and a wall!

"Miaooow!" she cried. Joe and Sally ran off to get Dad. They needed his help to rescue Tabby.

"Dad, come quick!" they shouted. "Tabby is in real trouble. She's just fallen off the roof!" Joe brought a cat carrier, and Dad carried a special pole with a loop on the end of it.

Sally looked worried. "That won't hurt her, will it, Dad?" she asked.

"No, she just won't like it very much," said Dad, "but it's the safest way to catch her and pull her free." Dad squeezed his arm into the gap behind the cowshed. "I think I need to go on a diet," he joked. "You two had better make sure I don't get stuck as well!"

"Don't worry, Dad," said Joe. "We would rescue you."

After a few tries, Dad slipped the loop over Tabby's head, and gently pulled her towards him. She was crying and wriggling, as Dad put her into the cat basket.

"Right!" said Dad. "Let's take her to the surgery." Tabby sat on the examination table, while Dad gently checked her all over.

"Luckily, no bones broken," he said. Joe and Sally sighed with relief. Then, he used a special instrument to look in Tabby's ears. "But she has got a nasty ear infection," he said. "That would have made her dizzy. I'll give her some pills to make her better, and we'll keep her indoors for a little while."

"No more Charlie-chasing for you," said Sally, giving Tabby a big cuddle later that day.

"Not yet, anyway," Tabby thought to herself as she settled down, curled up on Sally's lap in a comfortable armchair. She was very pleased with all the fuss, and purred happily. Before too long, Tabby was fast asleep.

Luckily, she didn't notice Charlie peeking in the window, to see if she was all right. Happy that Tabby was going to be fine, Charlie strutted back to the henhouse, and very quietly crowed... "Cock-a-doodle-doo!"

Being quiet wouldn't be too hard. Well, until Tabby was back to her good old self!

Ducks for a Day

One hot, sunny day, Becky and Bobby Chick waddled down to the stream, in search of some fun. They saw Duck swimming by. "Be careful by the water, chicks," she quacked, cheerily.

"We will, Duck," said Becky, watching the big duck swim gracefully past. "Oh, I wish we could swim, Bobby. It must be nice to be a duck."

When the little chicks spotted a large leaf bobbing gently up and down in the reeds, they just had to hop on for a game, even though they knew they shouldn't. "Let's pretend we're ducks!" laughed Bobby.

The two little chicks played happily on the leaf all morning. "Quack, quack! I wish we could paddle far away like real ducks!" laughed Bobby, jumping up and down. Suddenly, the leaf broke free of the reeds, and floated downstream!

"On, no!" cried Bobby. "How are we going to get off? We can't swim, we're not ducks! Help! Help!" The leaf-boat floated along, past the meadow where all the animals from Buttercup Farm were grazing.

"Don't worry, Becky, the farm animals will save us!" cheeped Bobby, waving his wing, trying to get the animals' attention. "Help!"

"Oh look, everyone!" mooed Cow. "The little chicks are waving to us!" All the animals laughed, and waved their tails back—everyone except Duck. She could see the chicks' frightened faces, as well as the waterfall up ahead! The chicks were in danger.

"They're not waving!" she cried. "They're floating away!" And with that, Duck leapt into the water, and paddled after the chicks, as fast as she could! When she reached the leaf she tried to pull it to the bank but the current was too strong, and they were getting very close to the waterfall.

Then, Duck had an idea. "Quick," she quacked to the two chicks. "Hop on to my back!" Becky and Bobby leapt on to Duck's back, then Duck swam back upstream to safety.

When they reached the farm, they jumped off Duck's back, and thanked her for saving them. Mommy Hen was waiting, anxiously. "We're so sorry, Mommy!" cried Becky, rushing over to her. "We'll never disobey you again!"

"It was nice being a duck for a while!" sniffed Bobby. "But being a chick is better!"

"And much safer!" clucked Mommy Hen, giving them both a big hug.

Buried Treasure

Jim lived in a big old house with huge, rambling grounds. The house was rather spooky, and Jim preferred the grounds. He would spend hours kicking a soccer ball around the grass, climbing the old apple trees in the orchard, or just staring into the pond in case he might spot a fish. It was a wonderful place to play, but Jim was not really a happy child because he was lonely. How he wished he had someone to play with! It would be such fun to play soccer with a friend, or have someone to go fishing with. He had plenty of friends at school, but it was a long bus journey to his home and, besides, his school friends found his house so spooky that they only came to visit once.

One day Jim was hunting about in the back yard with a stick. He hoped he might find something interesting to examine. Every time he found a new creature, Jim would draw it, and then try to find out its name. So far, he had discovered eight types of snail, and six different ladybugs. As he was poking about under some leaves he saw something sticking out of the ground. It was a piece of metal, and Jim reached down and pulled it hard. Eventually Jim managed to pull it free. In his hand lay a rusty old key. It was quite big, and, as Jim brushed away the soil, he saw that it was carved with beautiful patterns.

Jim carried the key indoors, and cleaned and polished it. Then he set about trying to find the lock that it fitted. First he tried the old gate to the grounds that had been locked for as long as Jim could remember. But the key was far too small. Next he tried the grandfather clock in the hall. But the key did not fit the clock's lock. Then he remembered an old wind-up teddy bear that played the drum. Jim hadn't played with the toy for a long time, and he eagerly tried out the key, but this time it was too big.

Then Jim had another idea. "Perhaps the key fits something in the attic," he thought. He was usually too scared to go into the attic on his own because it really was scary. But now he was so determined to find the key's home that he ran up the stairs boldly, and opened the door. The attic was dimly lit, dusty, and full of cobwebs. The water pipes hissed and creaked, and Jim shivered. He began to look under a few dustsheets, and opened some old boxes, but didn't find anything that looked like it needed a key to unlock it. Then he caught sight of a large book sticking out from one of the shelves. It was one of those sorts of books fitted with a lock. Jim lifted down the book, which was extremely heavy, and put it on the floor. His fingers trembled as he put the key in the lock. It fitted perfectly!

He turned the key and the lock sprang open, releasing a cloud of dust. Jim slowly opened the book, and turned the pages.

What a disappointment! The pages were crammed with tiny writing, and there were no pictures at all. Jim was about to shut the book when he heard a voice coming from the book! “You have unlocked my secrets,” it said. “Step into my pages if you are looking for adventure.”

Jim was so curious that he found himself stepping on to the book. As he put his foot on the pages he found himself falling through the book. The next thing he knew he was on the deck of a ship. He looked up and saw a tattered flag with a skull and crossbones flying from a flagpole. He was on a pirate ship! He looked down and saw that he was dressed like a pirate.

The pirate ship was sailing along nicely, when suddenly Jim saw some dangerous-looking rocks in the water—and they were heading straight for them! Before he could shout, the ship had run aground and all the pirates were jumping overboard, and swimming to the shore. Jim swam, too.

The water felt deliciously warm, and when he reached the shore he found warm sand between his toes. He couldn't believe it! Here he was on a desert island. The pirates went in all directions, searching for something to make a shelter. Jim looked, too, and under a rock he found a book. The book looked familiar to Jim. He was sure he'd seen it somewhere before. He was still puzzling over it when one of the pirates came running towards him waving a knife.

"You thief, you stole my rubies!" cursed the pirate in a menacing voice. What was Jim to do?

Then he heard a voice call from the book, "Quick! Step back here!"

Without thinking twice, Jim stepped into the book, and suddenly he was back in the attic again.

Jim peered closely at the page from which he'd just stepped. "The Pirates and the Stolen Treasure" it said at the top of the page. Jim read the page and found he was reading exactly the adventure he had been in. He turned excitedly to the contents page at the front of the book and read the chapter titles. "Journey to Mars", he read, and "The Castle Under the Sea". Further down it said: "The Magic Car" and "Into the Jungle". Jim was thrilled. He realized that he could open the book at any page, and become part of the adventure, then he only had to find the book and step into it to get back to the attic again.

After that, Jim had many, many more adventures. He made lots of friends in the stories, and he had some narrow escapes. But he always found the book just in time. Jim was never lonely again.

Wibble and the Earthlings

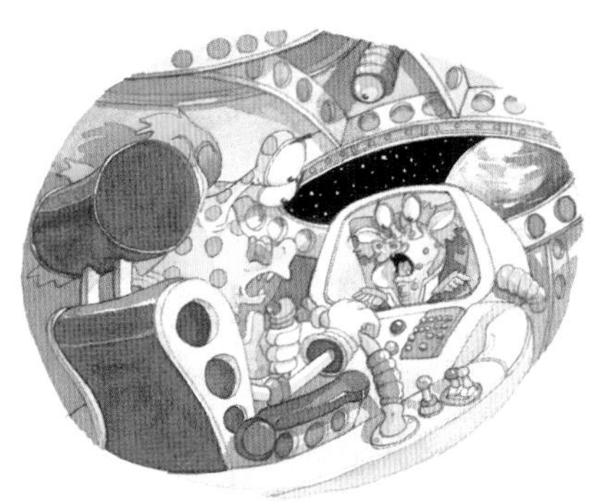

Wibble was from the planet Xog. He was on a mission. He'd been sent secretly to Earth to find out all about Earthlings. His spaceship wobbled on landing. There wasn't too much damage, but he had to radio back to Xog to tell them his camera was broken.

"Tell us what Earthlings look like," said Captain Pimples, the leader of the Xogs, "and I'll draw them. Over!"

"I will," said Wibble. "Over and out!" He climbed out of the spaceship and looked around. There was a big sign saying ZOO.

Wibble wobbled over to the nearest building and opened the door. He went up to a big wooden fence and saw his first Earthling. With its long neck, it leaned over the fence, and gave Wibble a huge lick. "Calling Captain Pimples! Calling Captain Pimples!" Wibble yelled into his radio. "This Earthling is friendly, and as tall as a tree! It has a long neck and little horns on its head! Over!"

Captain Pimples drew an Earthling with a very long neck, and two little horns on its head.

"Okay!" said the captain. "Tell me more. Over!"

Wibble wandered along to the next fence, marked ELEPHANT. He switched on the radio. "This one has huge ears, and a spout like a teapot! Over!"

Captain Pimples added the big ears and the spout to his drawing.

Next, Wibble went into the Aquarium. One tank had a sign that said SQUID. "This Earthling has two huge eyes, and is covered in orange spots! Over!" Wibble said into his radio. Captain Pimples added two huge eyes and orange spots.

"Okay!" said Captain Pimples. "We've heard enough. Earthlings are big, have enormous ears, a spout, two huge eyes, and orange spots. A bit like us really! Over and out!"

So Captain Pimples led an expedition to Earth. That is when Mr. Brown the Zoo-keeper walked by.

"Aargh!" cried the Xogs, and ran back to their spaceship. They took off and didn't stop until they reached planet Xog. Captain Pimples found Earth on his map, crossed it off, and wrote underneath, "BEWARE – MONSTERS!"

Birthday Bunnies

"It's my first birthday tomorrow!" announced Snowy, a little white rabbit, very proudly. "Isn't that exciting?"

"Yes, very exciting!" said Whiskers, her brother. "Because it's my birthday too!"

"And mine!" said Patch.

"And mine!" said Nibble.

"And mine!" said Twitch.

"I wonder if Mommy and Daddy have a surprise for us?" asked Snowy.

"I hope so!" said Whiskers, giggling.

Mrs. Rabbit was listening outside the door, as her children were getting ready for bed. She heard the little bunnies chattering excitedly about their birthdays the next day.

Whatever could she do to make it a special day for them? She sat and thought very hard, and later that evening, when Mr. Rabbit came home, she said: "It is the children's first birthday tomorrow, and I'm planning a surprise for them. I want to make them a carrot cake, but I will need some carrots. Could you go and dig up some nice fresh ones from your vegetable garden?"

"Certainly, dear," said Mr. Rabbit, and off he went.

Mr. Rabbit was proud of the carrots he grew. They were very fine carrots—crunchy and delicious. Every year he entered them in the Country Show, and they nearly always won first prize. So you can imagine his dismay when he arrived at his vegetable patch to find that every single carrot had been dug up, and stolen!

He marched back to the burrow. "Someone has stolen my carrots!" he told his wife, crossly. "And I am going to find out just who it is!"

And, although it was getting late, he went back outside, and set off to find the naughty person.

First of all he stopped at Hungry Hare's house, and knocked loudly.

"Someone has stolen all my carrots!" Mr. Rabbit said. "Do you know who?"

"Oh, yes," said Hungry Hare. "But it wasn't me." And, although Mr. Rabbit pressed him, Hungry Hare would say no more.

Next Mr. Rabbit went to Sly Fox's house.

"Someone has stolen my carrots!" he said. "Do you know who?"

"Oh, yes," said Sly Fox. "But it wasn't me." Although Mr. Rabbit begged and pleaded with him, Sly Fox would say no more.

So Mr. Rabbit marched to Bill Badger's house, and asked if he knew who had taken the carrots.

"Why, yes, in fact I do," said Bill Badger. "But it wasn't me."And just like the others, he would say no more. It was the same wherever Mr. Rabbit went, and, although he got very cross, and stamped his foot, no one would tell him who had stolen his carrots!

"You'll find out soon enough," said Red Squirrel.

So Mr. Rabbit went home feeling very puzzled.

"It seems that everyone knows who it was, but no one will tell me!" said Mr. Rabbit to his wife.

"Not everyone, dear," she said. "I don't know who it was either. All I know is that it's our children's first birthday tomorrow, and we have no surprise for them." And, feeling very miserable and confused, they went to bed, determined to get to the bottom of the mystery in the morning.

Next day the little bunnies came running into the kitchen, where their parents were having breakfast.

"Happy birthday, everyone!" called Snowy.

"Happy birthday!" cried the other little bunnies.

"Now, it's not much, but I wanted to give each of you a surprise!" Snowy went on. "By the way, I hope you don't mind, Dad." And with that Snowy pulled out a box of juicy carrots, each tied with a bow!

"Snap!" cried Whiskers, "I had just the same idea!" and he pulled out another box of carrots.

"Me too!" said Patch, and "Me too!" said Nibble. Soon there was a great pile of juicy carrots heaped on the kitchen table.

"So that's what happened to my carrots!" cried Mr. Rabbit, in amazement. "I thought they had been stolen!" And when he told the little bunnies the story they laughed till their sides ached. Then Mrs. Rabbit put on her apron and shooed them outside.

"Just leave the carrots with me," she said. "I have a birthday surprise of my own in store!"

And so the mystery was solved—it turned out that Hungry Hare had seen the little bunnies creep out one by one, and each dig up a few carrots when they thought no one was looking.

He knew it was their birthdays, and he guessed what they were doing. He had told the other forest folk, and everyone thought it was a great joke.

Mr. Rabbit felt very ashamed that he had been so cross with everyone, when they were really just keeping the secret. And so he invited them for a special birthday tea that afternoon, which the little bunnies thought was a great surprise.

And of course the highlight of the day was when Mrs. Rabbit appeared from the kitchen carrying, what else, but an enormous carrot cake!

Copycat Max

Max was a little tiger with a bad habit. He was a terrible copycat! He copied everyone, and everything. When the parrot squawked, "Pretty Polly, Pretty Polly," Max repeated it. "Pretty Polly, Pretty Polly!" Then, when the parrot got cross and said, "Shut up, Max, shut up Max," he repeated that as well. It was very annoying. One day, Max set off to explore. "I shall copy everything I see," he said to himself. And that's when the trouble really started!

First, he met a stork standing on one leg.

"How long can you do that for?" asked Max.

"Ages!" said the stork. "Only birds stand like this."

"Hmmm!" said Max, and lifted up one leg.

"Now lift up two more," said the stork. Max did, and fell in a heap on the ground. "Told you!" said the stork.

Then Max met a brown chameleon sitting on a green leaf. The amazing thing about chameleons is that they can change color when they want to. The chameleon saw

Max and changed his color to green, like the leaf—now he was invisible! Then he jumped on to a red flower, and turned... red!

"Watch this then," said Max, and he lay down on some grass. "Now I'm green," he said.

"Oh no," said the chameleon. "Only I change color."

"Hmmm!" said Max. He rolled in some mud. "Look," he said, "now I'm brown." Then he rolled in some white feathers. The feathers stuck to the mud. "Look," he said, "now I'm all white!"

Max decided to set off for home. He passed the stork still standing on one leg. The stork didn't recognize him. He arrived home late in the evening. His brothers and sisters were playing down by the river. They saw a white figure coming towards them.

"WOOoo!" wailed Max, pretending to be a ghost. "I've come to get you!" The tiger cubs were so scared, they rushed into the river and started to swim to the other side.

Max rushed in after them. Of course, the mud and feathers fell off in the water, and the others were really cross.

"It was only a joke!" said Max.

They agreed to forgive him if he promised not to copy anything again. "Oh, all right," said Max. And, for the moment, he meant it!

Going to Nursery

It was Monday morning. Jodie opened her eyes when she heard Mom coming up the stairs. "Time to get up!" Mom called, as she put her head round the door.

"Don't you want to go and see the nursery?"

"Yes, I do!" Jodie said. She wanted to find out more about the nursery that Mom had talked so much about. Jodie jumped out of bed, and Mom helped her to get dressed.

"Mom?" said Jodie. "What's it like at nursery?"

"Do you like climbing frames?" Mom asked her.

"Yes, I do!" said Jodie.

"Then you'll like nursery," Mom said. "There are lots of exciting things, like climbing frames, to play on. Come on, let's hurry up, and then you can see for yourself."

Dad was waiting for Jodie in the kitchen. "All ready to look at the nursery?" he said.

Jodie ate her cereal, and her toast. "I'm ready!" she cried. "Let's go!" When they arrived at the nursery, a lady was waiting to meet them. "You must be Jodie," she said, smiling. "I'm Mrs. Clark. Would you like to see what we do here?" Jodie nodded.

Mrs. Clark opened a door into a big room full of children having fun. Some of them were playing on a yellow climbing frame. Some of them were digging in the sand tray, with buckets, and spades. "Mom," said Jodie, "you were right. There are lots of exciting things to do at nursery."

Soon, it was time to go, but Jodie had so many questions about nursery. "When do I start?" she asked, on the way home.

"Next week," said Mom.

While she was eating lunch, Jodie said, "How long will I stay there?"

"Just for the morning, to start with," replied Dad.

Watching television with Mom that afternoon, Jodie asked, "Can I take teddy with me to nursery?"

"Of course," smiled Mom. "I think he'll enjoy it."

Next morning, Jodie and Mom went to the park. As Jodie was climbing up the slide, she met a small boy, who was standing at the top.

The little boy's mom smiled at Jodie's mom.

"He's starting at the nursery next week," she said.

"So am I!" cried Jodie. "What's your name?" she asked the boy.

"Jack!" he said, whooshing down the slide. "Do you like nursery?"

"I think so," Jodie told him.

"I'll see you there," said Jack, and he ran off, waving.

The week quickly passed and, at last, the day came for Jodie to start nursery. She was very excited, and a little bit scared, all at the same time.

"Where am I going to put my coat?" she asked Mom, as they pushed open the door of the nursery.

"They'll have your very own place all ready for you," said Mom.

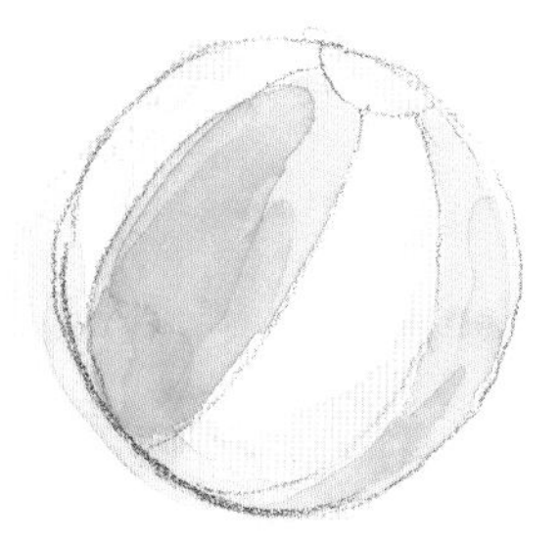

"Hello again, Jodie," said Mrs. Clark. "Can you see the hook for your coat? It's over here, the one with the blue peg. Now, what would you like to do first?"

Jodie noticed a boy, who was working on a big puzzle of a fire truck. It was Jack.

"Hi, Jack," she said. "Can I help?" She picked up a piece of puzzle and fitted it into place.

"I think it's time for me to go," whispered Mom, giving Jodie a hug.

"Okay, Mom," Jodie smiled. "See you later," and she picked up another piece of puzzle.

"Jodie's really good at this, isn't she?" said Mrs. Clark to Jack. Jack nodded—it was fun at nursery.

Then Mrs. Clark asked if they would like to help pass round the drinks and apple slices.

"Oh yes, please," said Jodie and Jack, together.

"Everyone, come and meet Jack and Jodie," said Mrs. Clark. All the girls and boys came over to say "Hello". Then Mrs. Clark asked Jodie and Jack what they would like to do next. Jodie knew exactly what she wanted to do. She tugged Jack over to the dressing-up box.

"Look!" she said, pulling out two big hats, "we could be firefighters."

Jack pointed to a big red car, standing in the corner. "And that could be our fire truck," he said.

After Jodie and Jack had put out lots of pretend fires, they saw two girls, busy making things at a table. They ran over to join them. There were boxes, and cardboard tubes, and glue, and paint everywhere.

"Let's make a fire truck," said Jodie.

Jodie started to glue two boxes together. She cut some card circles for wheels, and Jack helped her stick them on. Then, they painted the whole thing bright red.

Just as they finished, Jodie's mom slipped in through the door. Jodie ran over to her.

"Look! Come and see," she said, dragging Mom over to see the modelling table. "We made a fire truck."

"It's lovely!" smiled Mom. "Shall we take it home with us? It's time for lunch now."

Jodie put on her coat and waved to Jack. "Did you have a good time?" asked Mom. "Do you want to come again?"

"Yes, I do!" cried Jodie. "Nursery is great fun."

Fairy Fern

Deep in the heart of Rosebud Forest lives a tiny little fairy, with beautiful cobweb wings and a magic wand. The fairy's name is Fern, and her home is among the wild flowers that grow in a secret glade.

Fern has a special friend—Sapphire the bluebird. They love to fly through the forest, leaping over rays of sunlight, chasing pretty butterflies. Then, by the light of the moon, Sapphire and Fern dance and sing around a "fairy ring" with all their friends.

Today, Fairy Fern is really excited! There's to be a fairy parade. Flora, the Fairy Queen, will choose the prettiest fairy dress.

With a tap-tap of her wand, Fern magically changes into a dress of velvety rose petals and bluebells.

Then, with a sprinkling of fairy dust, Fern makes a secret wish... "Please let Queen Flora choose me!" she whispers.

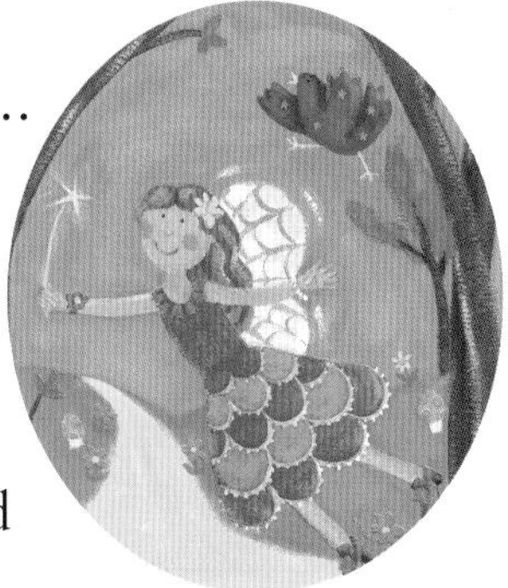

But Fern has forgotten to get her friend ready! She weaves some flowers through Sapphire's feathers, and adds a sprinkling of fairy dust.

Now for the final touch! Fairy Fern twists her hair up, and pins it into place with a golden flower. Then, with a flutter of wings, they fly off to the parade.

Fairy Fern arrives just as Queen Flora is announcing the winner... "and the Golden Crown goes to... Fairy Fern!"

All the fairies cheer and flutter their wings. Fairy Fern smiles as the crown is placed on her head. She is the happiest fairy in the forest—her secret wish has come true.

Maud and the Monster

Maud was a very cheerful but quite mischievous little girl. She also thought she was very brave. All the things which frightened other children were her favorites—slimy eggs, spider's legs, and even snails.

One day, as Maud walked past the basement door, she noticed that the light was on. Thinking of the fun she could have down there exploring, and playing games, she dashed down the stairs. But, as Maud reached the bottom step, she heard the door bang shut—and then the light went off! It was completely dark, and Maud began to feel rather frightened. She crept forwards, feeling along the wall, and peered slowly into the darkness. Round the corner she saw a bright, white monstrous shape! Maud screamed! The door burst open, the light came on and Maud's mom came rushing down the stairs, looking very worried.

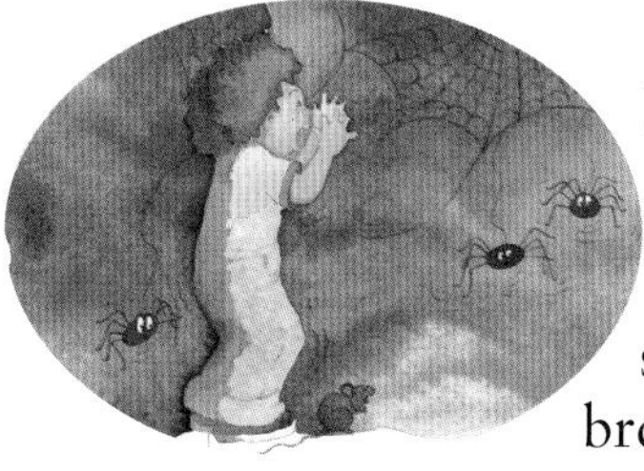

"Help, Mom! There's a monster!" cried Maud but then, as they both looked at where she was pointing, Maud realized it was the freezer!

Maud's mom laughed, and Maud felt rather silly. But after that she didn't boast about her braveness any more.

When Monsters go to Costume Parties

We all know what a costume party is, we dress up as something we are not—a pirate, a king, a princess, or a monster. Dressing up as a monster is especially good fun—you can make loud noises, and be rude, and blame it all on the monster. But what does a monster dress up as? Do they dress up like us? Do they put on their best clothes and think of polite things to say to each other? Do they make sure that they are well mannered, eat delicately and dance modestly?

Oh no! Monsters aren't any good at pretending, they gulp down their food in huge mouthfuls, and drop it all over the floor. When they dance they leap about, and stamp the floor until it shakes. They hate playing musical chairs because they slip and fall on the messy floor.

So monsters might go to a party dressed like us, but they cannot hide what's inside. They behave in a monstrous way—which I am sure you never do, do you?

The Smart Bear and the Foolish Bear

It was the start of winter. The first snow had fallen, and the lake had begun to freeze. It was time for all the bears to start their winter sleep. But there was one foolish bear who wasn't ready to sleep yet. "I'll just catch one more fish," he told himself, "to keep me going through winter." And, although he knew it was dangerous, he crept out onto the icy lake. He lay down on his tummy, and broke a hole in the ice. He could see lots of fish swimming in the water below. He dipped his paw into the hole, and scooped out a fish in a flash! But the foolish little bear leapt up, shouting, "I caught one!" With a great crack, the ice gave way beneath him, and he fell into the freezing water!

Luckily a smart little bear cub heard his cries. He found a fallen log and pushed it over the ice. The foolish bear grabbed it, and pulled himself to safety, still holding the fish.

"How can I thank you?" he asked.

"That fish would do nicely," said the smart little bear, and he strolled away with the fish to start his winter's sleep.

Crocodile Smiles

"Say cheese!" said the photographer. "CHEESE!" grinned Snappy the crocodile. Lights flashed, and cameras clicked as he gave his most winning smile.

"You're a natural!" cried the expedition leader. He was with a team of wildlife photographers. Snappy smiled at his reflection in the river.

Snappy was terribly proud of his sharp fangs, and fine good looks. He strutted up and down the river bank for all to see.

"I'm a star!" he said. "My face will be known throughout the world!"

"Thanks for letting us take your picture," said the expedition leader.

"No problem," said Snappy. "Any time!"

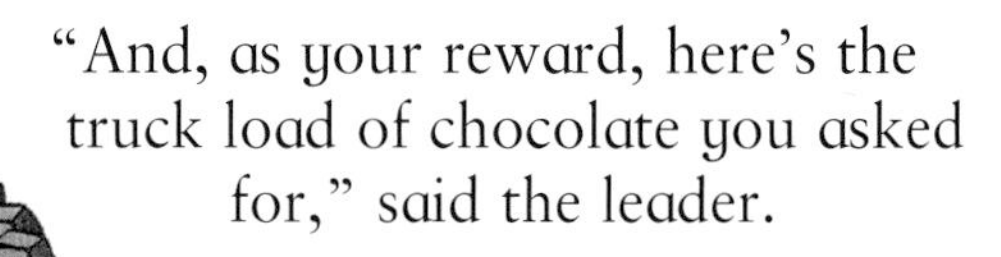

"And, as your reward, here's the truck load of chocolate you asked for," said the leader.

"How delicious!" said Snappy. "Most kind of you. Thank you so much."

When they had gone, Snappy lay sunning himself on the river bank, daydreaming of fame and fortune, and popping chocolate after chocolate into his big, open mouth.

Just then, along slithered Snake.

"What's thissss?" he hissed. "A crocodile eating chocolate? How very sssstrange!"

"Not at all!" snapped Snappy. "All crocodiles love chocolate. It's just that most of them aren't clever enough to know how to get hold of it."

"Well, if you're so sssmart, you ssshould know that too much chocolate will make your teeth fall out!" hissed Snake.

"What rot!" said Snappy, crossly. "For your information, I've got perfect teeth."

"Lucky you!" said Snake, and slithered off into the bushes.

So Snappy carried on munching happily, eating his way through the mound of chocolate. He had chocolate for breakfast, chocolate for lunch and chocolate for dinner.

"Ooh, yummy!" he grinned, licking his lips. "This is heaven."

"You won't be saying that when you are too fat to float in the river," said Parrot, who had been watching him from a tree.

"Nonsense!" scoffed Snappy. "I have got a very fine figure, I'll have you know!"

"If you say so," said Parrot, and flew off into the jungle.

Days and weeks passed, and Snappy happily carried on eating chocolate after chocolate, until at last it was all gone.

"Back to the river to catch my next meal, then," Snappy thought miserably. "Though I'd much rather have more chocolate!"

But, when Snappy slid into the river, instead of bobbing gently at the surface, he sank straight down, and his stomach rested on the bottom, in the mud.

"Oh, what's happened to the river?" Snappy wondered aloud. "It's very hard to float in today."

"Even for someone with such a fine figure as you?" jeered Parrot, watching from the trees. Snappy didn't answer. He just sank further beneath the water so that only his two beady eyes could be seen, and gave Parrot a very hard stare.

The next morning when he awoke there was a terrible pain in his mouth. It felt like someone was twisting, and tugging on his teeth. "Oww, my teeth hurt!" he cried.

"Sssurely not!" hissed Snake, dangling down from a tree. "After all, you have sssuch perfect teeth!" and he slunk away again, snickering.

Snappy knew what he had to do. He set off down the river to visit Mr. Drill the dentist.

It seemed such a long, hard walk, and by the time he got there he was puffing and panting.

"Open wide!" said Mr. Drill, an anteater, peering down his long nose into Snappy's gaping mouth. "Oh dear. This doesn't look good at all. What have you been eating, Snappy? Now show me where it hurts."

"Here," said Snappy pointing miserably into his mouth, and feeling rather ashamed, "and here, and here, and here... "

"Well, there's nothing for it," said Mr. Drill, "they'll have to come out!" And so out they came!

Before long, another photography expedition arrived in the jungle.

"Say cheese!" said the expedition leader.

"CHEESE!" smiled Snappy, appearing from behind a tree. But, instead of a flash of cameras, Snappy met with howls of laughter, as the photographers fell about holding their sides.

"I thought you said Snappy was a handsome crocodile with perfect teeth!" they cried, looking at the leader. "He should be called Gappy, not Snappy!"

Poor Snappy slunk away into the bushes and cried. It was all his own fault for being so greedy, and eating all that chocolate.

"There, there," said Mr. Drill, patting his arm. "We'll soon fit you out with some fine new teeth."

And from then on, Snappy vowed he would never eat chocolate again!

Misery the Grumpy Fairy

Misery didn't have any friends. It was her own fault, she grumbled all the time. One day Misery told the fairy who baked the bread, "Your bread is too soft. I like crusty bread."

"If that's your attitude," said the baker fairy, "you can bake your own bread." "I shall!" said Misery.

The next day she was rude to the fairy who mended her shoes.

"No one speaks to me like that!" said the cobbler fairy. "From now on you can mend your own shoes." "I'll be glad to," said Misery grumpily.

Then she insulted the fairy who collected the honey from the honeybees. "How dare you?" said the fairy. "I'm not staying here to be insulted. You can collect your own honey." And she stormed off. Soon there was no one in the village who would do anything for Misery.

"How will you manage?" asked Willow, her niece.

"No problem," said Misery. "I shall do everything myself." And she set to work to bake some bread.

Misery lit the fire, then she mixed and kneaded the dough, then she left it to rise. Then she put the loaf in the oven, and sat down for a well-earned rest. But, Misery fell asleep until a smell of burning woke her! All that was left of the loaf of bread were a few burnt cinders. What Misery didn't realize was that the baker fairy used a special baking spell—a spell that Misery didn't know!

Next Misery went to collect honey from the bees. She waved her arms at them, shouting, "Out of my way, bees." Their answer was to swarm around her, and sting her. What Misery didn't know was that the honey fairy used the special honey-collecting spell! She ran from the bees as fast as she could and, as she did, she lost her shoe! What a state she was in... burnt bread, bee stings on her nose and chin, and only one shoe!

"You can't go on like this," said Willow, when she saw her. Misery did some serious thinking. "Tell all the fairies I've turned over a new leaf," she told Willow. "From now on I shan't be a grumpy fairy any more."

Willow was delighted! So were the other fairies. Misery didn't complain about anything for months after that, and Willow kept her fingers crossed that it would last!

Fred the Fearless Fireman

Fireman Fred hurried to the fire station. It was his turn to cook lunch for the firemen on his shift, and he had just bought some nice, plump sausages at the butcher's.

At the fire station, Fred bumped into Builder Benny, who had come to repair a broken window frame.

"Oops! Hello, Benny!" he said. Then he went straight to the kitchen to start cooking. The smell of sausages wafted through the fire station. "Mmm, those sausages smell good!" said Dan and Mike, the other firemen, as they arrived for work. Suddenly the alarm bell rang—CLANG! CLANG! CLANG!

"Emergency!" cried Fireman Mike. He and Fireman Dan rushed down the pole, and into their fire-fighting gear. "What about the sausages?" cried Fireman Fred.

"Don't worry about a thing," said Builder Benny, coming in through the window. "I'll look after them till you get back."

"Thanks, Benny!" said Fireman Fred, trying to get his apron off as he rushed down to join the others.

The emergency was in Tony's Pizza Parlor. One of the ovens had caught fire!

"We'll soon have that blaze out!" said Fred, rushing in with a big fire extinguisher. Dan and Mike followed with the hose.

With a WHIIISH! and a WHOOOSH! from Fred, and a SPLIISH! and a SPLOOOSH! from Mike and Dan, the fire was soon out.

"Thank you!" said Tony, as the firemen took their equipment back to the truck. "I can get back to baking pizzas now!"

Just when they were ready to go back to the station, the firemen heard a call coming through over their radio. "Emergency! Emergency! Window cleaner in distress on Pine Avenue. Emergency! Over... "

"We're on our way!" said Fireman Fred, starting the truck. "Over and out!"

With sirens blaring, the fire truck zoomed into Pine Avenue. A crowd had gathered around Tip-Top Towers, the tallest building in town.

"It's Will the window cleaner!" cried Millie Mail Carrier, who had just finished delivering the day's mail to the building. "His ladder has broken, and he's hurt his leg. Now he's stuck, and he can't get down! Can you help him?"

"I certainly can!" said Fireman Fred. "I can be up there in no time!"

The firemen put up their tallest ladder. While Mike and Dan held out a net—just in case—Fred fearlessly began scrambling up the ladder. "Here I come, Will!" he shouted.

"I've got you!" said Fred, as he grabbed hold of the window cleaner. The crowd below cheered as Fred carried Will down the ladder, and helped him into the fire truck.

Fred drove the fire truck straight to the hospital.

"Thank you for rescuing me," Will said to Fred.

"Don't mention it," said Fred. "I'm sure your leg will be fine—but you will need a new ladder!"

"What a busy day it's been!" said Fireman Fred, as they drove back to the fire station. "I feel really frazzled!"

"Our work's not over yet!" said Fireman Dan. "Look! There's smoke up ahead!"

NEE-NAW! went the siren. VRROOOM! went the truck, as it raced to the scene of the fire.

The smoke was coming from the fire station!

Dan and Mike unwound the hose, and Fred raced inside. "Oooof!" he gasped, as he tripped over the hose and bumped into Benny—again!

"Sorry, fellows," said a red-faced Builder Benny. "I guess I burnt the sausages. I think your lunch is ruined."

Poor Fred felt really frazzled now—until he had an idea. "I know just the person to rescue us from this situation!" he said.

"Who?" asked the others. "Tony!" said Fireman Fred.

"His pizzas are yummy, and an extra-large one will be a perfect lunch for all of us!"

Monty the Mongrel

Monty was a very curious puppy. He liked nothing better than exploring the yard. "Don't go far," Mommy would say. But Monty wasn't worried about getting lost. He was a very good explorer.

One day, a big truck pulled up outside the house where Monty and his family lived. Men began carrying things out of the house. One of them said something about moving, but Monty was just a puppy, and didn't know what that meant. One of the men left the gate open so, when no one was looking, Monty crept out. He had a wonderful time sniffing around other people's yards. He found lots of yummy things to eat, and some really lovely things to roll in.

After a while, Monty began to feel tired. He was such a good explorer that he sniffed his way home with no trouble. But when he got there, he couldn't believe his eyes. Everyone, including Mommy, and all his brothers and sisters, had gone! Monty was very surprised, but he wasn't too worried. After all, he was a very good explorer.

He began sniffing at once, and soon found himself in the park where he met a group of dogs.

“What are you?” asked one dog.

“Well, he’s not a Poodle,” sniffed another dog, who Monty couldn’t help thinking looked like a ball of cotton wool. “He’s far too rough.”

“He’s definitely not a Dachshund,” said a third dog. He walked around Monty, and stared at him from all sides. Then he stopped. “Do you know what? I think he’s a MONGREL.”

“Well, if that’s the case,” sniffed the cotton wool dog, “he’d better hang out with Tinker.”

“Take no notice of them,” said Tinker. “They’re just trying to help.”

Monty gave Tinker a lick, and he told Tinker about his family.

“Let’s walk around the park,” said Tinker. “If we follow our noses, we might find your family.”

In the park, Monty sniffed the air. He could smell a very familiar smell. Suddenly, a huge brown dog bounded out of one of the houses on the other side of the park.

“Mommy!” shouted Monty.

“Monty!” barked Mommy. “Thank goodness you’re safe.”

“So you’re a Great Dane puppy,” laughed Tinker. “Not a mongrel, after all.”

Small and Pink

One morning, Percy the pig strutted proudly through the farmyard. "Today's the day," he told everyone he passed.

"What is he talking about?" asked Doris the duck.

"Percy is expecting some piglets," clucked Jenny the hen.

"I didn't think boy pigs had babies," said Doris, looking puzzled.

"No, no," Jenny clucked, flapping her wings. "They are coming from another farm to live here as part of his family."

Doris smiled. "Like Tilly and George and their new foal?" she said. "Oh, how lovely."

Percy had tripped and trotted

from one end of the farmyard to the other more times than he cared to remember, but Old MacDonald still hadn't returned with the new arrivals.

Percy went back to his sty one more time, and checked everything once again. It was spotless. The straw was piled up neatly along one wall, and the water trough was clean and full. Even the ground had been swept clean by the helpful mice!

"I must make sure that everything is ready for my piglets," said Percy, brushing a speck of dust from the doorway.

Just as Percy finished cleaning, brushing, and tidying he heard Old MacDonald's truck rumbling into the farmyard—they were here at last! All the cleaning and tidying had been worth it, here was his new family, and Percy was feeling very proud.

Percy was so excited! He hurried from his sty, but before he could reach the truck...

Whoosh! Something very small, very pink, and very fast shot past his nose. Then whizzz! Something just as small, and pink, and even faster scuttled under his tail. And then wheeeee! Another small, pink, and noisy thing zoomed straight under Percy's tummy even faster than the last two.

There was a flurry of pink legs and tails rushing in every direction, and with it came a burst of squealing and shrieking!

"What's going on?" gasped Percy, as he spun round on his trotters.

"Eeeeeeeeee!" shrieked seven little piglets. They were soon dashing all over the farmyard, in and out of everything at great speed. All the other animals gave up trying to keep up with them, and just watched in amazement. It seemed as if the arrival of the piglets had changed life for everyone, and they all wondered if they would ever have any peace again!

Late that night, a very tired Percy stood at the doorway of his sty— it was a tip. The straw was everywhere, and the water trough was upside down. But seven little piglets were fast asleep in the corner.

"Tired, Percy?" asked Jenny the hen.

"Yes," sighed Percy.

"They never stand still from morning till night, do they?" added Maria the sheep.

"No," sighed Percy.

"Are you having second thoughts, Percy?" asked Old George the horse.

But Percy gave the kind of grin that only a very happy and contented proud pig can give. "Shhhhhhh!" he whispered. "My babies are sleeping!"

Old Everest

Everest was one of the biggest and strongest horses in the world. When he was young, and already twice as big as other horses, he pulled the heavy cart filled with everything grown on the farm. He took the farm vegetables down to the market, and he brought things from the market back to the farm. He pulled the huge machine that cut the wheat to make flour. He pulled the big plough that dug the soil, so the farmer could plant the seed that grew into wheat that made the flour... that Everest took to market. He did everything!

"So why don't you still do everything now?" asked Puff the Pig.

"The farmer thinks I'm too old," said Everest, sadly. "He is trying to be kind. He thinks I need a rest."

Jacob the Lamb said, "I bet you are still stronger than anything, Everest! Nothing is as strong as you!" The huge horse lowered his head.

"Well... I am not as strong as I was, little one," smiled Everest. "Anyway, farmers don't use horses any more. They use a tractor instead!"

The big old horse spent most of the time now in his favorite meadow nibbling grass, and, when he grew bored with that, chasing rabbits or chickens. But if Parsnip the Sheep, Waddle the Goose, or Scratchitt the Cat were in his field, he would tell them his stories. Sometimes he told the same stories again without realizing, but no one minded.

Then one day the farmer said to Everest, "That tractor of mine! It won't start! I would ask you to help, Everest, but I suppose you are enjoying your rest." Everest shook his head from side to side.

Everest nudged the farmer gently over to the barn where the tractor was kept. His reins and harness were there too. The big horse picked up an old lead in his mouth, and hooked it on the front of the tractor. Then, as easily as anything, he pulled out the tractor. Then he pulled the plough up behind the tractor.

"You mean you can pull both together?" said the farmer. Everest nodded his head up and down. The farmer was amazed! So the farmer hooked the plough to the tractor. Then he hooked the tractor to the horse. And Everest pulled the tractor, and the tractor pulled the plough. Together they ploughed the field in the fastest time ever.

Everest was still the biggest, and the strongest... and now the happiest horse in the whole world.

Witches on the Run

At night, when it's all dark and scary, as you peek out over the bed covers, you might see shapes on the wall that will give you a fright!

If you think about it for too long, it just gets worse—you can hear the ear-piercing cackles and screams of witches, and the bubbling of their cauldron. If you look really hard, you can see the cauldron glowing with a strange light as the witches cast their spells. They stir the dreadful mixture with a huge wooden spoon, adding slimy green bits. And as you lie there, the smell from the spell gets stronger, and the bubbling gets louder!

But there is one thing on the planet that all real witches hate, and that is anything that is clean, particularly clean children! Of course witches never wash, and the thought of children with clean skin makes them feel very ill. They much prefer to be smelly and grimy.

So, the next time you think there are witches flying on your ceiling, remember all you need is clean skin, and they will vanish as quick as a flash!

Lonely Hearts

A lonely troll decided that he had to find a mate. This is the advert he put in the local paper:

Fun-loving troll, dirty and smelly,
With damp slimy skin, and big hairy belly
Nice muddy fingers, and grubby wet toes,
Hot steamy breath, and rings through each nose.

With stains on his shirt, and holes in his socks,
Teeth that need cleaning, and knots in his locks,
Tears in his pants, and scuffs on his shoe.
He's waiting to meet someone lovely like you.
He likes dirty ditches, and hiding in holes,
Is certain to win when he fights other trolls.

Is very attentive, will woo you with roses,
After he's used them to pick both his noses!
He lives on his own, in a dark stinking pit,
Oozing with slime, and covered in spit.
Now feeling lonely, he hopes there's a chance
He can meet someone similar for fun and romance!

Do you know anyone who will reply?

King Neptune's Day Off

Trini the little mermaid worked in King Neptune's palace. It had fountains and a statue of King Neptune in the courtyard. Trini was happy working there, but some fierce sharks guarded the palace.

On his birthday King Neptune called Trini to see him. "I'm taking the day off," he said. "I'd like you to organize a birthday banquet for me this evening. So, until then, you will be in charge." And off he went!

The sharks were delighted! They thought they would have some fun while King Neptune was away.

"I'm in charge, so you must do as I say," Trini told them, but the sharks sniggered, and swam away.

Trini set to work. She asked a team of fish to collect shrimps and special juicy seaweed. She told the crabs to collect smooth, pearly shells to use as plates. Then she sent her mermaid friends to collect pieces of coral to decorate the tables. But the sharks were determined to spoil everything. Soon they saw the fish carrying a net of delicious food.

"Give us that," they snapped, and ate the food. As soon as the crabs came back with their shell plates, the sharks took them and threw the plates to each other. Then the sharks started to chase the mermaids round the courtyard.

"Stop!" cried Trini. But they laughed and carried on. So Trini decided to trick the sharks! While they were having great fun chasing the mermaids, Trini squeezed through a crack in the hollow statue of King Neptune. The mermaids dropped all their pretty coral and swam away—the sharks couldn't stop laughing. They gathered around King Neptune's statue to plan some more mischief.

Suddenly, a voice like thunder boomed, "Behold, it is I, King Neptune, Emperor of all the Seas and Oceans. Do as Trini commands or you will be banished from the kingdom!" The sharks were very frightened. Then the voice from inside the statue told the sharks to pick up the plates and fetch more food, and lay the tables for the banquet. And, while they were busy, Trini crept out of the statue where she had been hiding!

So Trini's banquet was a great success. The sharks had to guard the palace, while everyone else had fun. King Neptune had a marvellous time and asked Trini if she would always be his special helper.

"I'd be delighted," she answered, blushing!

The Lost Lion

Once there was a lion cub called Lenny. He was a very tiny lion cub, but he was sure that he was the bravest lion in the whole of Africa. When his mother taught her cubs how to stalk prey, Lenny would stalk his mother and pounce on her. When she showed them how to wash their faces, Lenny licked his sister's face so that she growled at him. When the mother lioness led her cubs down to the watering hole to drink, he jumped into the water and created a huge splash that soaked everyone.

The other lionesses were not amused. "You'd better watch that son of yours," they said to Lenny's mother, "or he'll get into really big trouble."

One day the mother lioness led her cubs on their first big hunt. "Stay close to me," she said, "or you could get hurt."

She crawled off through the undergrowth with her cubs following on behind, one after the other.

Lenny was at the back. The grass tickled his tummy and he wanted to laugh, but he was trying hard to be obedient. So he crawled along, making sure he kept the bobbing tail of the cub in front in his sight. On and on they crawled until Lenny was beginning to feel quite weary.

"But a brave lion cub doesn't give up," he thought to himself. And on he plodded.

At last the grass gave way to a clearing. Lenny looked up, and to his dismay he saw that the tail he had been following was attached, not to one of his brothers or sisters, but to a baby elephant!

Somewhere along the trail he had started following the wrong tail and now he was hopelessly lost. He wanted to cry out for his mother but then he remembered that he was the bravest lion in all of Africa. So what do you think he did? He went straight up to the mother elephant and growled his fiercest growl at her.

"That'll frighten her!" thought Lenny. "She won't dare growl back!"

And, of course, she didn't growl back. Instead she lifted her trunk and trumpeted so loudly at Lenny that he was blown off his feet and through the air and landed against the hard trunk of a tree.

Lenny got up and found that his knees were knocking.

"Oh my," he thought, "that elephant has a very loud growl. But I'm still definitely the bravest lion in all of Africa." He set off across the plain. It was getting hot in the midday sun and soon Lenny began to feel sleepy. "I'll just take a nap in that tree," he thought, and started climbing up into the branches.

To his surprise, he found that the tree was already occupied by a large leopard. "I'll show him who's boss," thought Lenny, baring his tiny claws.

The leopard raised his head to look at Lenny, and then bared his own huge, razor-sharp claws. He took a swipe at Lenny with his paw. Without even touching Lenny, the wind from the leopard's great paw swept Lenny out of the tree and he landed with a bump on the ground.

When Lenny got up he found that his legs were trembling.

"Oh my," he thought, "that leopard has big claws. But I'm still definitely the bravest lion in Africa." He set off again across the plain. After a while he began to feel quite hungry. "I wonder what I can find to eat," he thought. Just then he saw a spotted shape lying low in the grass. "That looks like a tasty meal," thought Lenny as he pounced on the spotted shape. But the spotted shape was a cheetah! Quick as a flash, the cheetah sprang away and, as he did so, his tail gave Lenny a blow that sent him spinning round and round in circles.

When Lenny stopped spinning, he got up and found his whole body was shaking.

"Oh my," he thought, "that cheetah is a fast runner."

Then he added in rather a small voice, “But I’m still the bravest lion in Africa.”

He set off again across the plain. By now it was getting dark and Lenny was wishing he was at home with his mother, and brothers and sisters. “I wonder if they’ve noticed I’ve gone,” he thought sadly as a tear rolled down his furry cheek. He felt cold, and tired, and hungry as he crawled into the undergrowth to sleep.

Some time later Lenny was woken by a noise that was louder than anything he’d ever heard before—louder even than the elephant’s trumpeting. It filled the night air and made the leaves on the trees shake. The noise was getting louder and louder, and the animal that was making it was getting nearer and nearer. Lenny peeped out from his hiding place and saw a huge golden

creature with big yellow eyes that shone in the dark like lamps. It had a great crown of shaggy golden fur all around its head and its red jaws were open wide revealing a set of very large white fangs. How it roared! Lenny was terrified and about to turn tail and run, when the animal stopped roaring and spoke to him.

"Come here, Lenny," said the animal gently. "It's me, your father, and I'm going to take you home. Climb up on my back, little one."

So Lenny climbed up on his father's back and was carried all the way home. And when they got there his father told his mother and his brothers and sisters that Lenny had been a very brave lion after all.

Lizzie and the Tractor

Little Yellow the tractor came to a halt next to Lizzie the cow. The farmer leaned out of the tractor cab.

"Come on Lizzie, get up!" said the farmer. "We have the big farm show in one week. How are you going to win the Best Cow prize if you laze around all day getting plump? You're so lazy!"

"I like lying here!" said Lizzie the cow. "I have all the grass I need right here next to me. I don't even have to get up!"

The farmer did not know what to do. He thought the other animals might know how to make Lizzie lovely again, so he drove Little Yellow around the farm. Gorgeous the pig said, "Paint her pink with brown spots... it works for me."

Reckless the goat said, "She eats far too much grass. Get her to eat newspapers... it always works for me!"

When Little Yellow said he knew what to do, the animals just roared with laughter! But the farmer just said, "Please do everything you can, Little Yellow!"

So Little Yellow bustled around in his barn, trying on all the bits and pieces that a tractor uses. First he put on his big bulldozer bucket, went over to Lizzie, and scooped her up and took her into the field in the bucket. "It's for your own good," said Little Yellow.

Then Little Yellow put on his plough and ploughed up the grass in the middle of the field. The next day, Little Yellow ploughed another strip so that the ploughed bit got bigger and the grassy bit was smaller. Then Little Yellow put on his grass cutter and mowed all the grass that was left. Lizzie was smaller now, and the exercise was making her coat glossy.

Next Little Yellow put on his back forks and took Lizzie a bale of hay but, as she rushed to eat it, he drove away, and she had to trot behind to keep up. By the end of the day she was very tired, but fit and healthy too.

By this time, Little Yellow had used nearly every tool he had! The last thing he used was a power spray to wash her down, and... Ta-ra!... there stood Lizzie, more beautiful than ever before!

Lizzie went to the show, and of course was declared Best Cow. The farmer was given a silver cup to put on his sideboard. And all thanks to Little Yellow the tractor!

Bears Ahoy!

One summer's day, three little boys went for a picnic by the bank of a river. They took with them their swimming things, some cheese and pickle sandwiches and, of course, their teddy bears.

When they arrived, they found a small boat tied to a tree. The boys climbed on board, taking their teddies with them, and had a great game of pirates. The boys pretended to walk the plank, and soon they were all splashing about, playing and swimming in the river. They chased each other through the shallow water, and disappeared along the river and out of sight.

Now, the three bears left on board the boat did not get on very well together. Oscar was a small, honey-colored bear. He was good friends with Mabel, who had shaggy brown fur, but neither of them liked Toby. He was bigger than they were, and he was a bully. He was always growling at the other bears and telling them what to do.

As soon as the boys were out of sight, Toby leapt to his feet. The boat rocked. Oscar and Mabel begged him to sit down.

"I'm a fearless sailor," cried Toby. "I've sailed the seven seas and now I'm going to sail them again."

Before the others realized what he was doing, Toby had untied the boat, and pushed it away from the bank making the boat lurch about.

"Come on, crew. Look lively!" shouted Toby. "Do as I say or I'll make you walk the plank."

Now that it was untied, the little blue boat began to drift out into the river. It turned sideways gently, then caught the main current and began to gather speed.

"Toby!" cried Oscar. "We're moving!"

"Of course we are, you big softie," growled Toby. "We're bold and fearless pirates on the high seas."

Oscar and Mabel clung together in fright, as the little boat sailed down the river, past fields and houses. "Help!" they shouted. "Toby, make it stop!" But Toby was having a great time.

"Ha, ha," shouted Toby. "This is the life!"

Oscar glanced over the side. He wished he hadn't. The sight of everything passing by so quickly made him feel seasick.

"Look out, Toby!" he cried. "We're going to hit the bank. Quickly, steer it away before we crash!"

But Toby did nothing. He simply sat and watched as the little boat careered along, gathering speed as it headed for the bank. Oscar and Mabel clutched the sides of the boat tightly, and clung on fast. They were feeling very frightened. The boat hit the bank with a thump and Toby fell forward. The boat swung round, and headed for the middle of the river once more.

"Toby!" shouted Mabel. "Save us!"

But Toby was sitting in the bottom of the boat, rubbing a big bump on his head.

"I can't. I don't know how to sail a boat," he whimpered, feebly. He hid his face in his paws and began to cry. The boat zig-zagged on down the river, with the little bears clinging on to the sides in fright. In time, the river became wider and they could hear the cry of seagulls.

"Oh, Toby," cried Mabel. "We're heading for the sea. Please do something, quickly!"

"Nobody likes me," wailed Toby. "Now we're going to sink to the bottom of the sea, and you won't like me either!"

But Oscar wasn't listening. He had found a rope hanging from the sail. "Let's put the sail up and see if it will blow us to shore," he said.

"We'll be blown out to sea," wailed Toby, but Oscar ignored him, and carried on. The wind filled the sail and the little boat started moving forward. They sailed right across the bay to the far side, and blew up on to the beach.

"Oh, Oscar, you are a hero!" sighed Mabel, hugging him tight. "You saved us!"

Imagine the bears' surprise to see the three little boys running towards them along the beach—they had gone to find the coastguard and raise the alarm. There were hugs and kisses all round when they found the bears safe and sound. And you can be sure that, from that day on, Toby was a much wiser and kinder bear, and he never bullied the others again.

The Fluff Monsters

This is the story of the Fluff monsters. Everyone has seen fluff under the bed. That's because the Fluff monsters live under beds. They only come out when it's dark because they think it's scary during the day. Once, Fluff-boy was quietly eating fluff and custard, when suddenly the magic-sucking thing appeared. It made a terrible noise, then a tube with a brush on the end sucked up all the fluff after he'd spent ages collecting it!

Fluff-boy had only ever lived under his bed and he wanted to know what it was like under other beds. "Only naughty Fluff monsters go out in daylight," said Fluff-mommy, "and the Little Girl will get you!"

Fluff-boy's eyes opened wide. "Who's the Little Girl?" he asked.

"She's is a monster who lives in the bed," said Fluff-mommy. "She is really clean and pretty! She will wash you, and put you in a room filled with sun shine, and fresh air from outside!"

"That's horrible! I don't believe you," said Fluff-boy. "The Little Girl doesn't scare me!"

"You'll find out," said Fluff-mommy.

One night, while everyone was asleep, Fluff-boy wandered into the next room and found another bed to slide under. There were spiders and daddy-long-legs, cobwebs, and lots of fluff—perfect! So Fluff-boy sat and ate some fluff in his new home. But Fluff-boy couldn't sleep, he was thinking about the Little Girl. Plucking up courage, he carefully climbed up the bed covers. Suddenly, the Little Girl woke and sat up. Fluff-boy jumped with fright.

"Aaargh!" screamed the Little Girl, then they stared at each other.

"You gave me a fright!" said Fluff-boy.

"Me frighten you?" said the Little Girl. "You frightened me!"

"Did I?" said Fluff-boy. "Why?" laughed Fluff-boy. "I'm Fluff-boy. I've just moved in under this bed. Do you live in this bed too?"

"No, silly," said the Little Girl. "I just sleep here at night. I thought scary Bogeymen lived under the bed. But you're not scary at all!"

"How about this then?" asked Fluff-boy, and he pulled his scariest face. The girl laughed.

"That's not at all scary!" she said. "This is scary," and she pulled *her* scariest face. And that's how Fluff-boy and the Little Girl found there is nothing scary under the bed or in it!

The Dragon who was Scared of Flying

Once upon a time, in a land far away, there lived a dragon named Dennis. He lived in a cave high up in the mountains. All his friends lived in caves nearby, and his own brothers and sisters lived right next door. Now you would think that Dennis would have been a very happy dragon, surrounded by his friends and family, wouldn't you? Well, I'm sorry to say that Dennis was, in fact, a very unhappy and lonely dragon.

The reason for this was that Dennis was scared of flying. Every day his friends would set off to have adventures, leaving poor Dennis behind on his own. Dennis would stare out of his cave at the departing dragons. How he wished he could join them!

After they had gone, he would stand on the ledge outside his cave, trying to build up the courage to fly. But, as soon as he looked over the edge, he felt all giddy and had to step back. Then he would crawl back into his cave defeated and spend the rest of the day counting the stalactites on the ceiling or rearranging his large collection of bat bones.

Every evening, the other dragons would return with amazing tales of what they had been up to that day. "I rescued a damsel in distress," one would say.

"I fought the wicked one-eyed giant and won," boasted another.

"I helped light the fire for a witch's cauldron," announced a third.

"What have you been up to?" Dennis's sister Doreen used to ask him.

"Oh... um... this and that," Dennis would reply mournfully, looking down at his scaly toes. Then Doreen would lead him out of the cave and try to teach him to fly. Dennis would take a running jump and flap his wings furiously, but his feet would stay firmly on the ground. Then the other dragons would laugh so much that, in the end, he always gave up.

One day, Dennis could stand it no longer. The other dragons flew off as usual to find adventure but Dennis, instead of retreating into his cave, set off down the mountain side. It was very tiring having to walk. Dennis had never really been further than from his cave to the ledge and back, and soon he was puffing and panting. He was about to rest at the side of the path when his eye was caught by something colorful in the distance. Down in the valley he could make out some brightly colored tents, and now he could hear the faint strains of music drifting up to him. "I'd better take a closer look," thought Dennis. "Maybe I can have an adventure, like the other dragons!" He got so excited at the thought of his very own adventure that he started to run.

At last Dennis reached the tents and found himself in a world more exotic than he could ever imagine. He was surrounded by creatures such as he had never seen before. There was a yellow creature that roared, and another one with stripes and fierce teeth. There were also quite a few hairy creatures with long tails. Can you guess what all these creatures were? Of course, Dennis had never seen a lion, or a tiger, or a chimpanzee before. He thought they were very peculiar! The animals thought Dennis was

very odd, too. They stood in a circle around him. "How strange," snarled the lion. "A slimy thing with wings!"

"Look at its funny, knobbly tail," giggled the chimpanzees.

Dennis began to feel unhappy and unwanted again, but at that moment he heard a friendly voice saying, "Hello, there! Welcome to Chippy's Circus. I'm Claude the clown. How do you do?"

Dennis turned round. Now he felt really confused, for standing behind him was a man with the unhappiest face Dennis had ever seen. He had great sad eyes, and a mouth that was turned down so far that it seemed to touch his chin. Yet he spoke so cheerfully!

"I'm Dennis the dragon," said Dennis.

"A dragon, eh?" said Claude. "Well, we've never had a dragon in the circus before. Might be quite a crowd puller! Would you like to join the circus?" he asked.

"Oh, yes please," cried Dennis.

"Good!" said Claude. "I'm sure you're very talented," he added.

So Dennis joined the circus and was happy for the first time in his life. The other animals became friendly when they knew what he was. Claude taught Dennis to ride the unicycle and to do acrobatic tricks. He also learned how to dive into a pail of water. He didn't mind that a bit because his slimy skin was quite waterproof!

Now, as you know, dragons are particularly good at breathing fire, so Dennis soon became the circus's champion fire-eater. Folk would come from far and near to see Dennis shooting flames high into the dark roof of the big top.

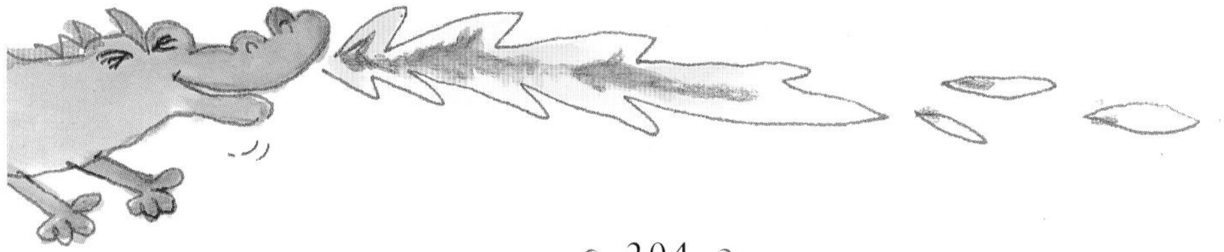

One evening, when Dennis had finished his fire-eating act, he sat eating an ice cream to cool his hot throat, and watched Carlotta, the tight-rope walker. She was pirouetting high up on the rope as usual. Then all at once she lost her footing, and Dennis saw to his horror that she was going to fall. He dropped his ice cream and, without thinking, flapped his wings furiously. As Carlotta fell, Dennis found himself flying up towards her. He caught her gently on his back and flew down to the ground with her clinging on tightly. The crowd roared and burst into applause. They obviously thought it was all part of the act.

"Thank you, Dennis," whispered Carlotta in Dennis's ear. "You saved my life."

Dennis was overjoyed. Not only had he saved Carlotta's life, he had also learned to fly. And then he said with a grin, "I do declare that flying is actually rather fun!"

Susie and the Mermaid

Today was Susie's birthday. Mom and Dad had given her a pretty sea-blue dress, and shoes which shimmered like a mermaid's tail.

Susie went to sit on Mermaid Rock and gazed out to sea dreaming of what it would be like to be a mermaid. "I'll make a birthday wish," she thought, and closed her eyes. "I wish I could be a mermaid." When she opened her eyes, she was no longer wearing her birthday dress—she had a mermaid's tail! Susie couldn't believe it, her birthday wish had come true!

Then Susie heard someone crying and saw someone wearing a blue dress just like her birthday dress! "Why are you crying?" Susie asked.

"I've lost my tail," the little girl replied. "I'm a mermaid but without my tail I can't go home!" Susie realized what had happened, her birthday wish had swapped her with the mermaid. Susie explained to the mermaid.

"If you collect my tears from the sea, then you could wish again and change us back," said the mermaid.

Susie slipped into the sea. With her strong new tail she swam quickly to the bottom of the sea.

Susie asked the sea creatures to help her search for the tears. Crabs and fish, lobsters and winkles peered into holes and lifted up stones, but it was no use. They couldn't find any tears. Susie didn't know what to do!

Then she heard, "One-two-three, one-two-three..." and an octopus appeared wearing a string of pearls! Its eight arms whirled around as it danced and twirled.

"Can you help me?" asked Susie. "I'm looking for mermaid tears."

"Ah! Well these pearls are just what you are looking for!" said the octopus. "That's what happens to mermaid tears you know—they turn into pearls! You can have them if you help me take them off!" laughed the octopus. "Oh, thank you so much!" cried Susie untangling the pearls.

Susie swam back to Mermaid Rock with the pearls, then she closed her eyes and wished. Instantly, she was wearing her blue dress and the mermaid had her tail back.

"Thank you, Susie," said the mermaid. "I hope that I'll see you again."

Susie waved goodbye as the mermaid slipped into the sea and swam away. Susie hurried home for her birthday tea. She glanced down at her new blue dress to make sure it was still clean. Down the front of the dress were sewn lots of tiny tear-shaped pearls!

Daisy the Dizzy Calf

One day, two special visitors were brought to Haven Farm—a poorly cow called Annie and her calf, Daisy. Sally and Joe helped their Dad settle them into the warm, comfortable barn. "You'll be fine now you've come to stay with us, Annie," said Joe, as he stroked the cow's soft nose. Sally gave the little calf a cuddle. "And you'll love it here, Daisy," she said. "Dad will soon make your mom much better."

That morning, Joe and Sally took Daisy into the meadow to meet the other animals. At first, Daisy found everything was a bit scary. The chickens ran in and out of her feet. The horses were enormous and the pigs were very noisy. Billy the goat was very, very bouncy all the time.

He skipped, jumped and bounced everywhere! "Don't be afraid, Daisy," said Sally. "Billy just wants to play." The little calf wanted to join in, but her wobbly legs just wouldn't do what she wanted them to! Billy gave her a playful nudge. Then, he bounced and skipped away to join the other animals. Poor Daisy was left stumbling after him.

"Don't take any notice, Daisy," said Joe. "He's just showing off!"

The little calf watched all the other animals having lots of fun, playing together. "Maybe if I practice," she thought to herself, "I won't be so wobbly."

That afternoon, Daisy ran round and round the meadow, jumping over the little stream at the bottom. "Hey, look!" laughed Joe, as he and Sally watched. "What a dizzy calf Daisy is!" The other animals also found the dizzy calf funny. Daisy was sure that everybody was making fun of her and she didn't like it. All she wanted to do was to join in!

As she walked away from the others, she saw the gate to the meadow wasn't closed properly. "I bet if I walked out of the farm," Daisy thought to herself, "nobody would even notice that I was gone." So, while no one was looking, Daisy quickly squeezed through the gate and carefully made her way up the hillside.

With each step, Daisy moved further and further away from the farm, and it wasn't long before she was very tired, very hungry... and very lost! As Daisy climbed to the top of the hill, the skies darkened and big rain drops started to fall. Shivering with cold, the little calf ran to shelter under an old oak tree. Suddenly, bright flashes of lightning lit the sky and thunder rumbled all around the hills.

"Mom!" mooed Daisy. "Where are you?" But the little calf was all alone and nobody could hear her cries.

Later that afternoon, Sally and Joe went to the meadow, to see how Daisy was settling in. But, when they arrived, there was no sign of her.

"Can you see her, Joe?" asked Sally. They both looked round the meadow but Daisy was nowhere to be seen! "She's not here!" cried Sally. "Let's take Patch and look round the farm. He might be able to find her."

Patch the dog led Joe and Sally to the barn... then the milking shed... and then the chickens' pen. But still, they couldn't find Daisy. Suddenly, Patch started barking by the meadow gate. The children rushed over and saw that the gate had been left open. There were lots of muddy hoof prints everywhere.

"We'd better tell Mom and Dad that Daisy's run away!" said Joe.

Patch led Joe and Sally up the hillside, while Mom and Dad followed behind them. As Patch searched he ran with his nose to the ground...

in the bushes... over the rocks... and round the trees, sniffing for signs of Daisy. He ran faster and faster, and then, suddenly, he lifted his head and started to bark. Joe and Sally ran until they managed to catch up with Patch.

"Good boy!" cried Joe. "Go find Daisy!"

Patch ran on to the top of the hill. There, under the shelter of the big oak tree, they could see Daisy lying asleep.

Joe and Sally, Mom and Dad arrived under the tree, all breathless from the run up the hill. "Oh, Daisy!" puffed Sally, kneeling down by the little calf, "I'm so glad we've found you!"

Dad quickly made sure that Daisy was safe to move. Mom helped to wrap the warm red blanket around her, then Dad picked up the cold, tired calf and carried her carefully down the hillside.

Back at the farm, Dad checked Daisy very carefully and then made sure she was safely tucked up next to her mom, Annie.

Annie was feeling much better, and was relieved to have her little calf safely by her side again.

"What's wrong with Daisy, Dad?" asked Joe.

"She's just very tired and cold," he said. "Nothing that rest, food and an extra bit of care can't put right." Joe and Sally gave the little calf a big hug.

"Daisy, we were all so worried about you when we couldn't find you anywhere," said Sally. "Everybody missed you so much."

"I've been so silly," thought Daisy, as she snuggled right up to her mom, and saw Joe and Sally smiling at her. "I won't ever run away again."

Annie nuzzled her little calf. What a dizzy Daisy!

No One Like You

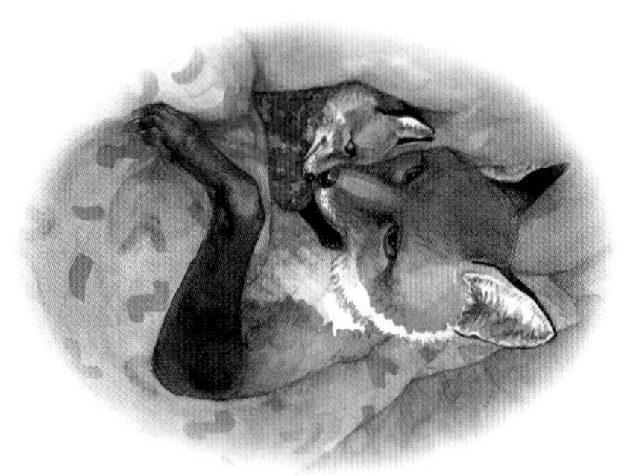

Ruff was hungry. A huge grumble rumbled in his tummy. He could hear Rufus clattering round in the kitchen. A delicious smell of freshly baked cupcakes sailed past his nose.

"Yummy," thought Ruff.

Ruff skipped into the kitchen—Rufus was washing up while the cakes cooled down.

"Would you like some help?" asked Ruff. "I could try one of those cupcakes for you."

"Oh, really!" said Rufus, smiling.

"No one makes cupcakes like you," said Ruff.

Ruff was bored. He twiddled his fingers, tapped his toes, and twiddled his fingers again. He had no one to play with.

Ruff was fed up. He was trying to make a model car. He fiddled and twiddled, but he couldn't put it together.

Then he had an idea! Ruff ran into the garden—Rufus was digging.

"Would you like something fun to do?" asked Ruff. "I could let you help me with my model car."

"Oh, really!" said Rufus, smiling.

"No one's as much fun as you," said Ruff.

It was bedtime! Rufus tucked Ruff into bed.

Ruff was feeling scared. He didn't like the shadows that flickered all round—it was very quiet. Then he had an idea! Ruff crept out of his bedroom and into Rufus' room.

Rufus was snoring loudly. It made Ruff giggle, which woke Rufus up.

"Would you like someone to cuddle?" asked Ruff. "I'm very good at cuddling."

"Oh, really!" said Rufus, smiling.

"No one cuddles like you," yawned Ruff, and he climbed into Rufus' bed.

"Oh, really!" said Rufus... "Well, no one loves you as much as I do, because there's no one like you."

Little Dog Lost

"Brrr," shivered Scruffy. "It's cold tonight."

"Well, snuggle up closer to me," said his mom.

"It's not fair," Scruffy grumbled. "Why do we have to sleep outside in the cold? The cats sleep inside, and they have nice warm baskets! I'd rather be a cat. All they do is wash themselves, eat and sleep."

"We're farm dogs, dear," said Mom. "We have to be tough, and work hard to earn our keep."

"We don't have such a bad life," said Mom. "Now stop feeling sorry for yourself, and get some rest. We've got a lot of work to do tomorrow."

The next day, Scruffy woke early and trotted down the lane for a walk. He ran through the grass, chasing rabbits, and sniffing at the flowers.

Now, usually, when he got to the end of the lane he stopped and turned back. But today, he saw a big red van parked outside a house there. The back of the van was open, and Scruffy thought he would just climb inside and take a look.

The van was full of furniture. At the back was a big armchair with

soft cushions. Scruffy clambered onto it.

"I could doze all day, like a cat!" he told himself. He closed his eyes and was soon fast asleep.

Scruffy awoke some time later with a sharp jolt.

"Oh, no, I fell asleep!" he groaned. "I'd better hurry back. We've got a busy day ahead!"

But then he saw that the van doors were closed! He could hear voices talking outside.

"Oh, dear, I'll be in trouble if I get found in here," thought Scruffy, and he hid behind the chair.

The back of the van opened and Scruffy peered out. Two men started unloading the furniture.

When Scruffy was sure that no one was looking, he crept out of the van, but he was no longer in the countryside where he lived! He was in a big noisy town, full of buildings and cars.

Poor Scruffy had no idea where he was!

"The van must have carried me away," thought Scruffy, feeling very frightened.

All day long, Scruffy tried to find his way home, feeling cold, tired and hungry. At last, he lay down and began to howl miserably.

"What's the matter, pup?" he heard a man's kindly voice ask him.

"You look lost. Come home with me." Scruffy gave the man's hand a grateful lick, then jumped up and followed him home.

When they arrived at the man's house Scruffy sat on the doorstep, hoping the man might bring out some food for him to eat. But the man said, "Come in, you can't stay out there."

Scruffy followed the man in, and found a little poodle waiting to meet him. Scruffy stared at her in amazement. What ever had happened to her fur?

"You'd better take a bath before supper," said the man, looking at Scruffy's dirty white coat. The man washed him in a big tub, then brushed his tangled coat. Scruffy howled miserably. What had he done to deserve such punishment?

"Don't you like it?" asked the poodle, shyly.

"No, I don't," said Scruffy. "I think that all this washing and cleaning is for cats!"

Next the man gave them supper—small bowls of dry pellets.

Scruffy looked at them and sniffed in disgust. He was used to chunks of meat and a nice big bone.

"This looks like cat food," said Scruffy, miserably.

After supper the poodle climbed into a big basket in the kitchen.

"I thought that belonged to a cat," said Scruffy. He tried sleeping in the basket but he was hot and uncomfortable. He missed counting the stars to help him fall asleep, but most of all he missed his mom.

"I want to go home," he cried, and big tears slipped down his nose.

The next day, the man put Scruffy on a leash and took him into town. He hated the way he was dragged along, without being able to stop and have a good sniff at things.

Then, as they crossed the market place, Scruffy heard a familiar bark, and saw his mom's head hanging through the window of the farmer's truck, parked by the side of the road! He started to howl, dragged the man over to the truck, then he leapt up at the window and barked excitedly. The farmer could hardly believe that this little dog was Scruffy—he had never seen him so clean!

The man explained how he had found Scruffy, and the farmer thanked him for taking such good care of him.

Scruffy and his mother leapt into the back of the truck. On the way back home, Scruffy told his mom all about his adventure and what had happened.

"I thought you must have run away because you didn't want to be a farm dog anymore," she said gently.

"Oh, no, Mom," said Scruffy, quickly. "I love being a farm dog. I can't wait to get home to a nice big juicy bone and our little bed beneath the stars!"

One Dark Night

Paws tiptoed out into the dark farmyard. Mommy had told him to stay in the barn until he was old enough to go out at night. But he was impatient. He had not gone far when something brushed past his ears. He froze as the fur on his neck began to rise. To his relief it was only a bat—there were plenty of those in the barn.

A loud hoot echoed through the trees—"Toowhit, Toowhoo!" and a great dark shape swooped down and snatched something up. "Just an owl," Paws told himself. "Nothing to be afraid of!" Creeping nervously on into the darkness, he wondered if this was such a good idea. Rustling sounds came from every corner, and he jumped as the old pig gave a loud grunt from the pigsty close by.

Then, all of a sudden, Paws froze in his tracks. Beneath the henhouse two eyes glinted in the darkness, as they came creeping towards him. This must be the fox Mommy had warned him of! But to his amazement he saw it was Mommy!

"Back to the barn!" she said sternly, and Paws happily did as he was told. Maybe he would wait until he was older to go out at night, after all!

The Night Carnival

Jim was a boy who hated the night, it made him feel lonely and gave him a fright. One night a bright light appeared outside, so he pulled back the curtains—and gasped in surprise...

There was a bright, shiny lantern outside his window! "It's carnival time!" cried the lantern, grinning. "Why don't you join in?"

"I'm on my way!" cried young Jim. With a skip and a jump he slid down the drainpipe and joined in the fun, dancing all night. But when it was time to go back to his room, Jim looked sad.

"Whatever is the matter?" asked the lantern.

"My room is full of monsters, and I'm scared of the dark," replied Jim.

"They aren't monsters at all," the lantern replied. "They are carnival folk—so there's no need to hide!"

The lantern and his friends left, and the room grew dark, but when Jim looked out from behind his hands he didn't see monsters, he saw carnival bands!

The Ghost Train

Hidden in the depths of the countryside, miles from anywhere, there is a very old, run-down railway station. But this is no ordinary railway station, the atmosphere is chilly, even on the warmest of nights...

Standing silently at the station is an old steam train that looks ready to leave. The carriages are full, there is a fireman, a guard and a driver. But when the guard blows his whistle the sound is an eerie shriek that will send shivers down your spine. As the wail of the whistle fills the air, the figures in the carriages begin to wave and shout from the windows—there is something very strange about them!

Their shapes become clearer in the glow from the station lights. They are witches, ghosts, goblins and ghouls, all waiting endlessly for the ghost train to pull out of the station silently, and chug slowly up the phantom line.

This is one train ride you won't want to take!

The Mermaid in the Pool

John and Julia were staying in an amazing vacation home with a big swimming pool. But, best of all, their bedroom overlooked the beach. The first night of the vacation there was a storm. The wind howled and waves crashed over the beach, right up to the house. The children sat on the bed watching the storm outside.

In the morning, there was seaweed all over the yard, and there was a mermaid swimming up and down the swimming pool! John and Julia rushed outside but, when the mermaid saw them coming, she huddled in a corner of the pool. "I'm sorry I swam into your blue pool," said the frightened mermaid. My name is Marina. I was playing in the sea with Blue, the dolphin, when the storm began. A huge wave washed me in, and now I'm stranded, and Blue is missing!"

"We'll help you look for Blue," said Julia at once. "We might be able to see your friend from our bedroom window."

When their mom and dad were safely out of the way, John and Julia found a wheelbarrow, and wheeled Marina into the house. "I've only had sky over my head," said Marina. "The house won't fall down will it?"

"Of course not," smiled John. They showed Marina all sorts of things she had never seen before. She thought Julia's teddy bear was wonderful, and that beds were the silliest things she had ever seen! But, although they looked out of the window, there was no sign of Blue the dolphin in the sea.

Marina explained that she couldn't stay out of the sea for too long. So John and Julia lifted her back into the wheelbarrow and pushed her down to the beach. They spent the rest of the day searching for shells along the seashore. Suddenly, Julia spotted a large shell half buried in the sand. John found a stick and dug it out.

"It's my shell!" cried Marina. They washed off the sand and Marina blew into it. The most beautiful sound drifted out across the waves and, straight away, there was an answering call! Far out to sea, they saw a streak of blue-grey leaping high over the waves, swimming towards them. It was Blue the dolphin! Marina gave a cry of joy and swam to meet him. She flung her arms round his neck and hugged him. Then she called to the watching children. "Thank you for helping me."

And they watched as Marina and Blue swam swiftly and smoothly together, back out to sea.

Millie the Mixed Up Mail Carrier

Millie Mail Carrier worked hard delivering letters, and she was always in a hurry. She hated to keep the people on her round waiting—and Mr. Price the Mailmaster always expected her back at the post office by 12 o'clock.

One morning Millie was in a bigger hurry than ever. She had overslept and was late for work! "Hurry, hurry, rush, and hurry!" Millie muttered to herself as she rushed out the door.

"People are waiting for their letters!" Millie Mail Carrier said to herself, as she sped to the post office on her bike. "And Mr. Price will be waiting for me!" She zoomed down the street as fast as her bike would go.

"Sorry I'm late, Mr. Price," Millie puffed as she flew through the post office door.

"Good morning, Millie!" said Mr. Price. "Your postbag is here— and it looks very full today!"

"Thanks, Mr. Price," said Millie. "I'll really have to hurry, with all those letters and parcels!" Millie sped down Main Street and around the corner of Jackson Road. She was going so fast that she didn't see the removal truck in front of her until it was too late! "LOOK OUT!" shouted the removal men. "Oh dear!" shouted Millie, as she flew off her bike. Everything in Millie's postbag went flying, too!

"Oh no! It will take ages to collect all these!" cried Millie, when she had stood up and dusted herself off, "and I'm in such a hurry today!"

The removal men helped Millie collect all the letters, postcards and parcels and put them back in her bag. It wasn't too long before she was ready to go.

But when Millie picked up her bike, she saw that the tyre was flat! "I've got a puncture!" she cried. "I can't ride this now. What will I do?"

"You'll have to walk your round today, Millie," said one of the removal men.

"Oh no!" said Millie. "I'm late enough as it is! I'd better get going!" Millie ran off to deliver the post as quickly as she could.

But she was in such a hurry that she got all the names and addresses mixed up!

Mr. Green, on Jackson Road, was expecting a parcel of books. Instead, he got two letters and a gas bill addressed to Mrs. Jackson!

Mrs. Jackson, who lived on Holly Drive, got a magazine that was supposed to go to Holly Walker!

And Holly Walker, who lived on Green Street, got the parcel of books meant for Mr. Green!

Everybody was terribly confused, especially Millie Mail Carrier!

"Oh no! I am getting so mixed up!" she exclaimed.

Millie rushed and hurried as quickly as she could to try and sort everything out... but by 11 o'clock her postbag was still half full.

She was beginning to feel hopeless, when suddenly she saw something that gave her a brilliant idea.

"Jack, may I borrow your skateboard, please?" Millie asked one of the children. "I promise to return it as soon as I've delivered all my letters."

"That's fine Millie," said Jack.

Millie had never been on a skateboard before, but she bravely stepped on. Millie wibbled and wobbled... and teetered and tottered... then she skidded and swayed... and WHOOOOSHED and WHIZZZED down the street.

"Wheeeeeeeee!" cried Millie with glee. "This is just what I need!"

Millie zoomed up and down the street at lightning speed. She had such a good time that the rest of her round seemed to get done very quickly.

"This is much faster than walking," she said, "and much more fun than my bike!"

At last Millie's deliveries were done. She returned the skateboard to Jack, and had just enough time to rush back to the post office.

"I'm back, Mr. Price!" she gasped, tripping over her bike as she staggered through the door. "Right on time!"

"I'm glad, Millie," said Mr. Price. "And I'm glad you're all right. The removal men brought back your bike. I guess we'll have to mend that puncture right away."

"Oh there's no hurry, Mr. Price," said Millie. "I think I've found a much better form of transport for a Mail Carrier like me!"

The Tooth Fairy

Pansy was nearly five. She couldn't wait for her birthday because Mom had promised her a party in the yard with a birthday cake, balloons, and a funny clown. But there was a problem! Pansy's two front teeth were loose, and very wobbly. How was she going to enjoy her party food?

That night Pansy woke suddenly. The curtains were open and her bed was covered in silvery moonlight. But that wasn't all! Sitting on Pansy's pillow was... can you guess? A fairy! She was tiny, with pale yellow wings, a wand, and a sparkly dress. Pansy could not believe it. She stared at the fairy, and the fairy stared back at her.

The fairy spoke first. "Can you see me?" she asked. "Yes," said Pansy.

"That's funny," said the little fairy. "Usually I'm invisible!" "Are you the tooth fairy?" asked Pansy.

"Yes, I'm Bobo," said the fairy. "I need two tiny front teeth to replace the keys on my piano." Pansy showed Bobo her two front teeth. They were very wobbly.

"I hope they come out before my birthday party," said Pansy.

"They'll come out when they are ready," said Bobo. "If they come out in time, I'll play my piano at your party!"

At tea time Bobo watched from behind a bowl of fruit, as Pansy ate all her cheese on toast, including the crusts. Still her teeth didn't come out!

"Try brushing your teeth," Bobo whispered to her before Pansy went to bed.

"Oh yes! That will do it!" said Pansy. And she brushed and brushed, but the wobbly teeth just stayed stubbornly in her mouth.

The day before Pansy's birthday her two front teeth came out! It didn't hurt one little bit. "Look!" she said to Mom, pulling a face, and showing a big gap where her teeth should be.

That night Pansy went to bed early and put her teeth under the pillow. The first thing Pansy did in the morning was look under the pillow. The two tiny teeth had gone! In their place were two coins.

Pansy's fifth birthday party was the best she'd ever had. All her friends came. There was jello and ice cream, balloons, and the funniest clown she'd ever seen. But only Pansy could hear the tiny fairy playing a piano and singing Happy Birthday in a silvery voice.

The Missing Scarf

Kanga was very proud of her stripy knitted scarf. She had made it herself and she had also made a smaller matching one for her son, Joey. Kanga used to hop through the bush with her scarf streaming out behind her, while Joey's could just be seen poking out of the top of her pouch. Now Joey was older, he was too big for Kanga's pouch, but he still wore his scarf as he hopped along beside his mother.

Then one day Kanga woke up to find that her beautiful scarf was missing. She searched high and low but it was nowhere to be found. Eventually she decided that she would have to go out into the bush to look for it.

"Stay here," she said to Joey. "I'll try not to be long. I'm sure to find my scarf soon." Kanga hopped off into the bush and started to search among the roots of trees and under stones.

She had gone quite a long way when, looking up into the branches of a eucalyptus tree, she spotted Koala. Now Koala was usually asleep, but this time she was preparing a meal of eucalyptus leaves for her children. Kanga looked up at Koala and then her jaw dropped. For Koala was quite clearly wearing Kanga's scarf around her tummy. Then, to Kanga's horror, she saw Koala use the end of the scarf to wipe the teacups! "Koala," Kanga called. "Whatever do you think you're doing?"

Koala stopped cleaning the teacups and looked down through the branches of the eucalyptus tree at Kanga. "I'm wiping my teacups with my apron," she replied sleepily, "and I'll thank you not to interfere!" And with that, she yawned and moved several branches further up the tree.

Poor Kanga felt very embarrassed. How could she have mistaken Koala's striped apron for her own scarf? She hopped away and carried on further into the bush. After a while she heard Kookaburra's familiar laughing call nearby. "I know," thought Kanga, "I'll ask her. She'd be able to spot my scarf easily from the sky." She followed the sound of Kookaburra's call until she came to the tree where she lived. Kanga was about to call up when her jaw dropped again. For Kookaburra was quite clearly carrying Kanga's scarf in her beak. "Kookaburra," Kanga called. "Whatever do you think you're doing?"

"I'm lining my nest," mumbled Kookaburra through a beakful of stripy feathers. "And please don't interfere," she added as she arranged the feathers carefully in place.

Poor Kanga felt even more embarrassed. She carried on further into the bush. After a while she reached a wide, open plain and there she saw Emu running past with his baby chicks on his back. As he rushed past, Kanga's jaw dropped yet again. Emu quite clearly had Kanga's scarf tucked in amongst his chicks.

"Emu, whatever do you think you're doing?" called Kanga.

"I'm taking my chicks to safety," said Emu, glancing up at the sky as he sped away. "And you should do the same," he added. Kanga realized that what she had thought was her scarf were just the striped chicks on Emu's back.

Poor Kanga felt even more embarrassed. Then she felt a few spots of rain on her nose.

Looking up, she saw a huge black cloud overhead—she must find shelter. She made a dash to the edge of the plain and soon found herself by a stream. She wandered along feeling cold, wet, tired, and miserable. Finally, she lay down in the wet grass beside the stream and tried to get to sleep. She shivered with cold and wondered how Joey was, and whether he was behaving himself. She so hoped he hadn't got into mischief.

Just then there was a tap on her shoulder and there stood Platypus. "I could hear you in my burrow over there," she said pointing towards a hole beside the stream just above the water. "I thought you might like this to keep you warm," she added.

"My scarf!" exclaimed Kanga.

"Oh, that's what it is! I'm ever so sorry," said Platypus. "I've been using it as a blanket for my babies. It's very cold and damp in my burrow, you know," she added, rather forlornly. "It was stuck on some thorns and I know I shouldn't have taken it, but I just thought it would be so nice for keeping my young ones warm," blurted Platypus, and she started to sob.

"There now," said Kanga, "please don't cry. You can keep the scarf. You need it more than me."

Platypus stopped crying and looked overjoyed. "Thank you," she said.

"No, thank you," said Kanga. "I've learned a lesson, which is not to get upset over a scarf, for I've ended up falling out with my friends."

Kanga made her way back home, but it took a long time because she apologised to all her friends on the way. When she explained what had happened Emu, Kookaburra, and Koala all forgave her, and by the time she reached home she was feeling much better. Joey was there to greet her. "What have you been up to while I was away?" she asked.

"I made you this," he said. He handed her a scarf. It was a very funny-looking scarf, made out of twigs, grass, and feathers, but Kanga loved it very much.

"This is much more special than my old scarf," she said. And she gave Joey an extra big hug.

Barney the Boastful Bear

Barney was a very boastful bear. "Look at my lovely soft fur!" he would say to the other toys. "See how it shines!"

Barney loved to talk about himself. "I'm the smartest toy in the nursery!" he would say. "It's a well-known fact."

He didn't know that the other toys all laughed about him behind his back.

"That bear thinks he's so smart," growled Scotty Dog. "But he isn't smart enough to know when everyone's really fed up with him!"

"He'll learn his lesson one of these days," said Molly Monkey, and sure enough, that is just what happened...

One hot summer's day, the toys lazed in the warm nursery. "Wouldn't it be lovely if we could all go for a walk outside," said Rag Doll.

"We could have a lovely picnic in the woods!" said Old Bear.

"Even better, we could all go for a drive in the toy car first!" said Rabbit.

"But none of us is big or clever enough to drive the toy car," said Rag Doll, sadly.

"I am!" came a voice from the corner. It was Barney. He had been listening to them talking.

"I can drive the toy car. And I know the best place for a picnic in the woods," he said.

"We've never seen you drive the car," said Rabbit, suspiciously.

"That's because I drive it at night, when you're asleep," said Barney. "I'm a very good driver, in fact."

"Ooh, let's go then!" cried Rag Doll. And in no time they had packed up a picnic and were sitting ready in the car.

"Er, I don't feel like driving today, actually," mumbled Barney. "It's too hot." But the others were not interested in hearing his excuses, so rather reluctantly Barney climbed into the driver's seat and started the engine. You see, the truth was, Barney had never really driven the car before, and he was scared. But he wanted to show off, so he pretended to know what he was doing.

Off they set down the garden path. "Toot, toot!" Barney beeped the horn as he turned the little car out into the country lane, and soon they were driving along, singing merrily.

All was going well, until Rag Doll suddenly said, "Hey, Barney, didn't we just miss the turning for the woods?"

"I know where I'm going," said Barney, crossly. "Leave it to me." And he made the little car go faster.

"Slow down a bit, Barney!" called Old Bear, from the back seat. "My fur is getting all ruffled." He was starting to feel anxious.

"I don't need a back-seat driver, thank you," said Barney, with a growl, and made the car go even faster. By now the others were starting to feel scared, but Barney was having a great time.

"Aren't I a wonderful driver!" he chuckled. "Look—no hands!" And he took his paws off the steering wheel. Just then they reached a sharp corner. The little car went spinning off the side of the road and crashed into a tree, tipping all the toys out into the ditch!

They were a bit dazed, but luckily no one was hurt. They were not pleased with Barney though.

"You're a silly bear!" said Rabbit, crossly. "We could all have been badly hurt!"

"We'll have to walk home now," said Rag Doll, rubbing her head. "Where are we?"

Everyone looked at Barney.

"Don't ask me!" he said, quietly.

"But you told us that you knew the way!" said Old Bear, indignantly.

"I was only pretending," said Barney, his voice trembling. "I don't really know how to drive, and I don't know where we are!" And he started to cry.

The other toys were furious with Barney.

"You naughty boastful bear!" they scolded. "Now see what trouble your boasting has got us into!"

The lost toys walked through the dark woods all night long, clinging together in fright as shadows loomed around them.

They had never been out at night before. Then, just before dawn, they spotted the little house where they lived, and crept back into the nursery.

What a relief it was to be home again!

Luckily their owner had not noticed they were missing, so she never knew what an adventure her toys had been having while she was fast asleep. She often wondered what had happened to her toy car though.

Puppy's Paw

One sunny day, a small puppy sat in a grassy yard, watching Snowball and Snowdrop, his brother and sister, play. His coat was white with a few brown patches—and he had one brown paw. When he was born, his mommy said, "He looks like he's forgotten to put his other socks on!" And that is how Socks got his name.

"Can I join in?" barked Socks.

"No, you can't!" Snowball yapped back, rudely.

"He looks like he's been having a mud bath, with those brown splodges," sneered Snowdrop. "Go and wash yourself properly, Socks."

"Maybe we should wash him," laughed Snowball. And the two puppies chased Socks towards the bird bath.

Socks ran off as fast as he could and hid inside the shed—why didn't they like him? Was it because he didn't look like them? A big tear fell from his eye and trickled down his nose. Then, the two bouncy puppies appeared.

"Socks, where are you?" barked Snowdrop. Socks peeped out from behind the shed.

"We're going to the wood for a walk, Socks," called Snowball. "Bye-bye!"

Socks couldn't help himself. He ran out on to the grass. "Please can I come?" he begged.

"You're much too young to come with us," said Snowdrop. "And you know Mommy says that you're too young to go out without her."

"I'm not too young," whined Socks. "I've been out loads of times."

"Well, you can't walk with us," said Snowball. "You must make sure you walk behind us."

"Okay," yapped Socks, eagerly. So, the two pups scampered through the yard gate, with Socks following. Snowball and Snowdrop ran down the lane towards the wood—Socks trotted behind!

In a clearing, there were two paths to choose from. Snowball's nose began to twitch. He could smell something wonderful. "This way!" he yelped, and the two older pups rushed off.

"Don't those two ever stop to look where they're going?" wondered Socks, as he lifted his brown paw and followed. Round a bend, the puppies found a huge clump of beautiful, pink flowers. Socks pushed his soft, black nose into them. "Atishoo!" he sneezed, as yellow pollen flew into the air.

Snowdrop was busy chasing a butterfly. It fluttered away down another path and Snowdrop followed. "Come on, Socks!" barked Snowball. "Keep up!" and he set off after his sister.

"We'll get lost if we're not careful," thought Socks.

The butterfly led the puppies deeper and deeper into the wood.

Suddenly, it flew high into the air and then it disappeared. Snowdrop and Snowball stopped and looked around. There were trees everywhere and they all looked the same!

"How are we going to find our way home now?" wailed Snowball.

"Listen," woofed Snowdrop. "There's someone through those trees. Let's see if they know the way home."

"I know the way... " began Socks. But Snowball and Snowdrop weren't listening. They had already dashed off along the path.

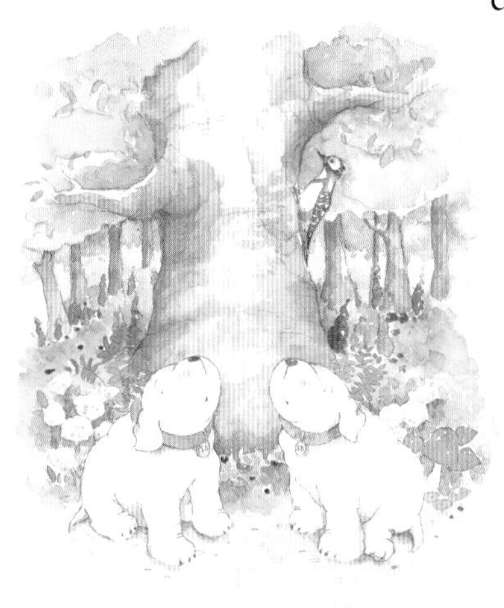

"It's easy," thought Socks to himself and set off after the others.

Tap-tap! Tap-tap! A woodpecker was trying to find some insects in a tree. "Can you help us find our way home?" asked Snowball and Snowdrop. But the woodpecker flew off!

"What are we going to do now?" whined Snowdrop. "I want my mommy!"

"Help!" they howled. "Help!"

"But I know the way home!" said Socks.

Snowdrop and Snowball turned to their brother and stared. "What did you say?" they asked.

"I said I know the way home," said Socks, again.

"How?" asked Snowball.

"It's easy," said Socks. "Every time we chose a path, we took the one on the side of my brown paw. To get home, we just turn round and take the path on the side of my white paw. Just follow me and I'll show you."

So, back through the woods they went, with Socks in front. Each time they had to choose, Socks held up his brown paw, turned his head, and took the other path. Back they scampered through the wood, past the pink flowers, down the lane, through the gate, and into the yard, where their mommy was waiting for them.

"Where have you been?" she woofed, crossly. "I've been so worried."

"We got lost," said Snowball and Snowdrop. "It was all our fault."

"Socks was so clever," woofed Snowball. "We're so lucky to have him as a brother."

"I wish I had a brown paw like him," said Snowdrop. "Do you want to play ball, Socks?"

"Oh, yes please!" he woofed, flicking the ball across the grass to his brother and sister. Sometimes it was good to be different!

A Good night Kiss

"It's bedtime now, Oakey," said Mom. Oakey curled up in the chair. His ears began to droop and he muttered, "Oh, that's not fair!"

"Have a drink first," smiled Mom, "then you must go."

Oakey's ears drooped and off he went. But he was back in a flash! "Where's your drink?" asked Mom. "You haven't been very long. You look scared, Oakey. Is there something wrong?"

"There's a monster in the kitchen, with long, white shaggy hair, lurking in the corner, behind the rocking chair," said Oakey.

Mom laughed. "Oh, Oakey, you've made a mistake. That's no monster. It's a mop." And she gave the mop a shake.

Oakey's ears drooped and off he went. But he was back in a flash! "What's the matter?" asked Mom.

"There's a ghost in the hallway, hovering around. Look, it's floating just above the ground," he wailed.

"Oh, Oakey, you've made a mistake. It's an old coat, hanging on the hook. Coats don't float!" laughed Mom.

Oakey went off to bed, slowly. But he was back in a flash! "Why aren't you in bed, Oakey?" asked Mom.

"There's a great big lump waiting beneath the sheets. I'm scared it's going to pounce on me," sniffed Oakey.

"Oh, Oakey, you've made a mistake. The only thing underneath the sheets is your old teddy bear," smiled Mom.

Oakey got into bed. But he didn't close his eyes. "Why aren't you asleep?" asked Mom.

"There are huge creepy crawlies underneath my bed," complained Oakey.

"They're just your slippers, Oakey. They won't be creeping anywhere without your feet inside," grinned Mom. "That's it now, Oakey. Time to say good night."

Mom switched off the light—then Oakey saw it by the door! It moved across the floor, straight towards him, with its arms stretched out, then it leaned over him and Oakey closed his eyes. What happened next gave Oakey an enormous surprise. The monster picked him up and cuddled him tight!

This couldn't be right! Then Mom's voice whispered, "Don't worry, it's just me. When I said 'Good night' just now, I forgot to give you this." Then Monster Mom gave Oakey a good night kiss!